STITCH HEAD

The Beast of Grubbers Nubbin

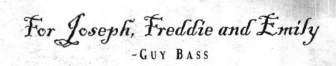

For Joseph, Freddie and Emily

-GUY BASS

For Phoebe

-PETE WILLIAMSON

STiTCH HEAD

The Beast of Grubbers Nubbin

Guy Bass

Illustrated by Pete Williamson

STripes

Guzzlin' Day

A Ye Olde Ode,
In the form of a poem,
By way of a rhyme

Greed is wicked, base and vile
But once a year it makes us smile
So bust a gut at our buffet
And stuff your face on Guzzlin' Day!

Self control's for lesser folk
So pack your gob until y' choke
Cram your maw! Eat like thunder!
Gobble down until y' chunder!

Gluttons rule for one day only
Wolf a horse! Pig out on pony!
Cow's-foot pie! Goat's-head soup!
Fill y' boots until y' poop.

When you're sated, don't stop eatin'!
Give your guts another beatin'!
If you can stand to leave the table
Guzzle up 'til you're unable!

WELCOME TO
GRUBBERS NUBBIN
(POPULATION 664)
Yesteryear

EVERYONE'S WELCOME
(Almost)

Ah, Grubbers Nubbin in the winter! Though the air was crisp and the fog was thick, the welcome was as warm as a log fire. Such gracious townsfolk! Such deep-filled pies! Such crooked smiles! Perhaps you'd have tickled your innards with a swift chug of neck oil down the Dog 'n' Trumpet, or supped a warming brew in Mrs Winkleberry's Olde Shoppe of Unspecific Teas. Why, you were as welcome as a belly-filling bowl of boiled broxy brains on Guzzlin' Day, the warmin' winter *feast*ival!

Unless, of course you were a *monster*. For the fine folk of Grubbers Nubbin knew what it was to live in fear of monsters, creatures and mad things. For as long as the town has been a town, so loomed Castle Grotteskew. High upon a hill stood the castle, casting its ominous shadow upon the town. Grotteskew was home to the maddest professor of all, Mad Professor Erasmus. Day after day, the professor toiled in his sinister laboratory, creating one unnatural horror after another, until the castle brimmed with monsters – and monsters were not welcome in Grubbers Nubbin.

But little did the troubled townsfolk know there were more than monsters in Castle Grotteskew… Hidden within its walls were creatures even more unpredictable, more unusual, more terrifying.

And they were all *hungry*.

LITTLE TERRORS

(No escape)

Monsters do not fear the dark
We creep and crawl at night
But the sound of Little Terrors
Is enough to give us fright

Signed,
The Creations of Grotteskew

"You hear that? The Little Terrors are coming," whispered Arabella. She was a scruffy girl of ten, with hair like a bird's nest and a fascination for all things mad and monstrous. Arabella stared at the old wooden door. "Say your prayers, Stitch Head."

"Maybe we could *hide*. Maybe there's still time..." came a whimpered reply. Stitch Head cocked his bald, ash-grey head, tracing his fingers across the patchwork of sewn-together features that made up his face. A distant, thundering rumble filled the air.

"There ain't no time for running and hiding," Arabella replied, the sound of the Little Terrors growing louder. She looked at the large brass bell clutched in Stitch Head's tiny hand. "You summoned them. There ain't no escape ... not for any of us."

"But ... but I don't know if I can do this.

I don't know if—" began Stitch Head, cradling the bell as the floor began to shake.

"Too late for that! Here they come!" Arabella cried.

BOOOM!

The door burst open and a tidal wave of human children flooded into the room. Their matching uniforms, once spotless and pressed, were already worn and threadbare from their first week at the castle. Their hair, once combed and neat, was now wild and unkempt.

"Ahh!" Stitch Head squealed, dropping the bell with a KLAANG! and scaling a tattered curtain to avoid the stampede.

In fact, despite his odd appearance, the children barely noticed him – but then Professor Erasmus's first creation had spent most of his life hiding in the shadows,

only coming out to cure his master's more unpredictable creations of their ferocity. He had a knack for not being noticed.

But Stitch Head could not hide from his responsibilities. the days of hiding were over. The Little Terrors were *his* problem – and he had to deal with them head-on.

"So *many* of them," he muttered. He watched the hundred orphans jostle for places around a long makeshift table, put together from seven smaller tables, and carefully laid with a hundred bowls and spoons.

"Well, if this ain't a sorry state of affairs, I don't know what is. Castle Grotteskew ain't no place for *humans*," sighed Arabella. She picked up the bell from the floor as the children squabbled for seats. "It's s'posed to be full of *monsters*."

"I'm sorry, Arabella ... but what else could I have done?" replied Stitch Head, dangling from the curtain. "I mean, their orphanage was run by an evil spider-lady who fed on their souls..."

"Yeah, and thanks to you, she's deader than doorknobs at the bottom of a lake," huffed Arabella, ruffling her already untidy hair. "I don't see why we 'ad to drag this lot back with us."

"We couldn't just *leave* them there," Stitch Head replied. "They had no one to look after them. They had no—"

"Yeah, yeah, *poor* little urchins," Arabella sneered. "The point is, I ain't hardly seen a single unspeakable horror all week! Even Pox refuses to come down from the ceiling…"

Stitch Head looked up to see Arabella's pet monkey-bat (half-monkey, half-bat) pacing along the hall's crisscrossing ceiling beams, yapping nervously.

"YaBBiT YaBBit! SWaaRTiKi!"

16

"See?" added Arabella. "I've seen him bite off his own toe, but even he ain't nutty enough to hang around with the Little Terrors. Every monster in the castle is in *hiding* since the Little Terrors arrived."

Stitch Head understood exactly why the creations had secreted themselves in the darker corners of the castle. The children were like a force of nature – a whirlwind of energy, noisy and unpredictable. Stitch Head felt so overwhelmed in the orphans' company that it was all he could do to stay in the room with them.

"I didn't think they'd be so ... spirited," he said, climbing gingerly down the curtain and hopping on to the floor next to Arabella. "A week ago, they were so quiet, but now—"

"Now they're noisier than a trump in a trumpet!" growled Arabella, slamming the bell on the table.

"At least we're not doing this alone," added Stitch Head, huddling behind Arabella's leg. "At least we have—"

BOOOM!

The door at the other end of the room flew open and a monstrous creature strode in. It was a ludicrously large combination of elements, with a long tail, a third arm and a single eye in the middle of its face. Atop its head it wore a tall white chef's hat, and in its two biggest arms it carried a cooking pot large enough to hold at least three sheep.

"AWFULS of Castle Grotteskew!" the Creature boomed, holding the pot aloft. "DINNER is SERVED!"

THE SECOND CHAPTER

HAIL TO THE CHEF

(The most tasteful taste you'll ever taste)

MAD MUSING NO. 453

"Gustation and Digestion are luxuries reserved for the less-than-mad."

From *The Occasionally Scientific Writings of Professor Erasmus Erasmus*

"It's food!" cried one of the children, as the Creature wielded the enormous pot. Excited murmurs began to ripple through the room.

"Real grub!" said another child.

"Mercy on me belly guts!" added a third.

"I've been licking the mud off my shoes for a week!" cried a fourth.

"The Creature did it… It actually *made* food," Stitch Head whispered in awe.

The Creature was one of Professor Erasmus's more recent creations – and its friendliness and positivity had been enough to convince even the most nervous orphan that there was nothing remotely monstrous about the monsters of Grotteskew. It was also one of the few creations that did not run and hide in the face of the Little Terrors' rampant youthfulness.

"Who's HUNGRY?" it hollered. The

hundred children cheered in deafening unison. "NO more eating ROTTEN fruit, BEETLES and those six dead CROWS I found in the chimney. TODAY you eat like QUINGS and KEENS!"

"The Creature's really building it up," Stitch Head whispered to Arabella. "That food must be *delicious*." Arabella raised an eyebrow suspiciously.

"PRESENTING the GREATEST culinary extravaganza since SLICED eggs!" the Creature continued. "The most TASTEFUL taste you'll ever taste! The FOOD that does you GOOD! I give you … STUFF!"

The Creature slammed the pot down upon the table, sending all one hundred bowls jumping into the air. The children cheered again.

"RIGHT, let's make sure you're all FED UP!" the Creature boomed. "SERVICE!"

"Yes, chef! Whatever you are saying, chef!"
came a cry. In an instant, the tiny figure of Ivo
came running through the door. Ivo was the
castle's oldest creation. He was no bigger than
a doll, with an egg-shaped head, a cloak of
rags, and a single rusty metal arm, in which,
at this moment, he carried an oversized ladle.

He hurried to the cooking pot but was far too small to reach the table, never mind the bubbling Stuff.

"Ivo?" said Stitch Head. "Since when is he the Creature's assistant?"

"Let's GO!" shouted the Creature. "The CHIEF has SPOKEN! I mean, SHOUTED!"

"It's 'chef', not 'chief', you dog-brain dope," Arabella shouted back. "And who d'you think you are, barking orders? Ivo ain't your slave!"

"I do not mind!" added Ivo, struggling to climb a table leg. "I spent ninety-eight years alone in very small dark room. I like to be shouted at! It means someone is paying me attention."

"There's so MUCH to CHIEFING," continued the Creature. "There's SHOUTING, HOLLERING, SCREAMING… I think I was MADE to be a chief. I've finally found my CALLING."

"I just can't believe you actually made *food*, Creature!" said Stitch Head. "None of the creations even need to eat – how did you know where to start?"

"CHIEFING is EASY when you have RAW talent like me – although I ALSO have BOILED, FRIED and GRILLED talent," the Creature replied.

"Yeurgh! What a stench!" howled Arabella, as she approached the pot.

"Stench?" repeated Stitch Head. "I can't smell anything…"

"I also have no smells," confessed Ivo, trying to catch a scent on the air.

"That's 'cause you two ain't hardly got *noses*," Arabella groaned, recoiling. "Trust me, that Stuff stinks worse than my nan did before her yearly scrub-down! I ain't going nowhere near it."

Stitch Head gave the Creature an encouraging smile, before clambering on to the table and peering anxiously into the pot. His eyes grew wide.

"Oh…" he muttered. "*No.*"

STUFF

(How to make the Stuff)

17 EYES (evil)

5 BRAINS

(undead/undying)

12 TENTACLES

15 ZOMBIE VAMPIRE BATS

TOP SECRET
RECIPE
(No peekings)

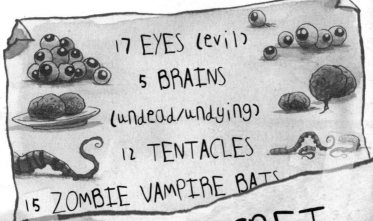

The pot was brimming with a mould grey stew. It bubbled and popped like molten lava, belching clouds of mucus-yellow dust into the air. Stitch Head had tried food before, even though he didn't need to eat, but he'd never even *seen* anything like this. No single ingredient of the concoction was recognizable as food. The stew's numerous ingredients squirmed like they were struggling to escape from each other. Tentacles writhed just beneath the surface. Eyes bobbed into view before vanishing into the ooze. A lone toe floated by. It was as if the Creature had given form to a terrible nightmare – and then imprisoned it within a cooking pot.

"This ... this looks like it belongs in the professor's laboratory," whimpered Stitch Head, a shiver of fear running down his borrowed spine.

"That's because it DOES!" replied the Creature gleefully. "I mean, it DID. I FOUND all these INGREDIENTS when I was going THROUGH the professor's DUSTBINS… You should SEE how much he THROWS away. SOME of it is still ALIVE!"

"Uh, what exactly is in the Stuff, Creature?" asked Stitch Head. By now the orphans too were retreating from the smell. "What's it made from?"

"A chef does not give away secret recipe!" insisted Ivo. "Also, I lost count of what went in pot after we add zombie vampire bats…"

"For added BITE!" declared the Creature. "Just TRY it, Stitch Head, you'll LOVE it!"

Everything told Stitch Head to run away to the darkest corner he could find … but then he looked up at the orphans. A hundred expectant, hungry faces stared back at him.

He had to set an example, to show the orphans they were safe … to prove to them he was right to bring them to Castle Grotteskew.

Stitch Head gripped the ladle tightly. The stew hissed like an angry cat as he dipped it into the churning mulch. The Stuff tugged upon it, pulling it in like a dog with a bone. Stitch Head struggled for a moment before wrenching the ladle out with a grunt. The stew farted like an old lady.

"THAT'S it, take a nice, BIG mouthful of SECRET flavours!" cried the Creature.

Stitch Head slowly brought the Stuff to his lips. Smoke puffed from the goo and a passing fly was overcome by the fumes. It spiralled into the ladle and was immediately swallowed into the sludge. Stitch Head retched involuntarily. He held his breath … and pushed the ladle into his mouth.

The glob of stew burst like a popping boil. It felt somehow both slimy and dry upon Stitch Head's tongue.

"What you think?" asked Ivo. Stitch Head cautiously smacked his lips together.

"It's … it's … it's…" he began, his eyes wide. "It's *not bad at all.*"

"YES!" cried the Creature. "I knew it! I'm the BEST chief EVER!"

"Actually," added Stitch Head, "once you get past the initial surprise, it's really quite a pleasaUUUUUURRRGH!"

A sudden torrent of grey-green vomit flew out of Stitch Head's mouth, exploding with such force he was sent flying into the air! Stitch Head whizzed around the room like a deflating balloon, propelled by his own foul expulsions. Arabella and the orphans ducked in horror as he whooshed over their heads, showering the room in unpleasantness.

"AAUUUURRRRGH—!" wailed Stitch Head, helplessly out of control.

"Is that a GOOD 'AAUUUURRRRGH'?" asked the Creature, hopefully.

"I am not sure there is such thing as a good 'Aauuuurrrgh'," replied Ivo.

"Somebody grab him!" cried Arabella, as the jet of vomit propelled Stitch Head straight towards a wall. "Stop him before—"

"AAUUUURRGH—"

KRUD.

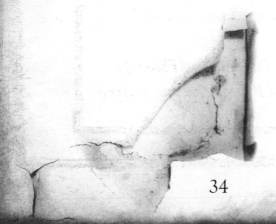

CUTHBERT
(Two keys)

"Stitch Head?"

Stitch Head opened an eye. He saw Arabella staring back at him, picking chunks of vomit out of her hair. He let out a queasy "*Urgh*," and sat up, holding his stomach.

"You all right?" she asked. "I didn't even know a body could have that much puke inside it."

"It look like your insides tried to get away from your outsides," added Ivo.

"So did you LIKE the STUFF?" asked the Creature, looming into view. "Shall we start SPOONING it out to the AWFULS?"

"No!" cried Stitch Head. "That is, I mean, you did your – *urgh* – best, Creature. But maybe you should put the Stuff out of harm's way for now?"

"What Stitch Head is *trying* to say is your grotty grub ain't good for nothing, except

maybe warding off the devil!" snapped
Arabella. "You couldn't even call it—"

"Food!"

Everyone turned to see one of the orphans
clamber on to the table. He was a plump,
copper-haired boy, no older than Arabella.
Like all the orphans, he wore the uniform of
the orphanage, but only his remained tidy and
unspoiled.

"Cuthbert…" sighed an anxious Stitch Head. Stitch Head had yet to learn all the children's names, but he couldn't help knowing Cuthbert. He was usually the first to speak, and always the loudest.

"Is it not obvious from our pallor, our frailty, our imploring looks that we orphans are *starving*?" Cuthbert cried. "We need food! F-U-D-E! Why, we haven't had a proper meal all week!"

"Oh, shut your spit-hole, *gobby*," Arabella snarled. "Ain't you had enough of the sound of your own yakking?"

"My *name* is Cuthbert, you mad thing. K-U-T-H-B-I-R-T," the boy replied fearlessly. "And I speak for all these neglected unfortunates you have seen fit to pluck from our home!"

"Home?" growled Arabella. "When Stitch Head rescued you, you were having your spirits

38

sucked dry by an evil spider-lady! Which was better than you deserved 'n' all."

"So you decided to bring us here, to a place of *monsters*?" continued Cuthbert, his arms clamped to his cheeks in mock horror. "A place of bolted windows and locked doors! Are ... are we *prisoners*, held hostage against our will? Oh, woe is we!"

"I don't UNDERSTAND a WORD he says," the Creature whispered to Ivo, as the orphans began to grumble in agreement.

"You ungrateful toenails! Would you rather be out there toiling in the workhouse?" roared Arabella. She took a large iron key out of her pocket and brandished it like a weapon.

"Fine!" she added. "I've got the key to the front door – let me show you out!"

"Arabella…!" whispered Stitch Head, as Cuthbert paced down the table. "We're supposed to be making them feel *welcome*."

"But even prisoners get fed!" continued Cuthbert dramatically. " And we are so very, very hungry!"

"I THINK he's trying to TELL us something," mused the Creature to Ivo. "But WHAT?"

A defiant cheer went up from the orphan throng, and they started banging their bowls on the table. Stitch Head opened his mouth to speak, but even if he could have thought of something to say, no one would have heard him over the orphans' disgruntled din. Did they think it was a bad idea to bring them here, too? And what did it mean for the creations

… and Professor Erasmus?

As the noise grew, Stitch Head's resolve faded. Despite himself, he started retreating towards the nearest shadow. He needed time to think … to plan … to find a way to make this *work*.

"Squit!" Cuthbert continued, and a small, bone-thin boy with grey eyes leaped to attention. Cuthbert pointed to the brass bell, still sitting on the corner of the dinner table. "Fetch me that bell! It's time for some ye olde school rabble-rousing…"

Arabella snatched up the bell before Squit could reach it.

"Oh no! You ain't getting this bell, you big—" she began, but when she looked down, her hand was empty.

"H-here you are, C-Cuthbert," he stuttered, handing him the bell.

"What the blinkin—?" blurted Arabella, staring at her empty hand.

"Oh, Squit here can steal your purse and plant a flower in your lapel without you even noticing," sneered Cuthbert. Then he rang the bell with all his might.

CLANG-A-LANG-A-LANG-A-LANG-A-LANG-A-LANG!

"We want food! We want food!" Cuthbert cried. The orphans were quick to join in.

"We want food! We want food!"

"I WISH they'd just TELL us what they WANT," whispered the Creature.

"Stop. Please, stop…" cried Stitch Head, but his voice was drowned out against the children's chanting. He held his hands over his ears and closed his eyes. It was more that he could take. "Stop … please…"

"Shut your noise-holes!" Arabella cried.

"We don't owe you nothing! Right, Stitch Head?"

Arabella turned, just in time to see Stitch Head race out of the dining hall.

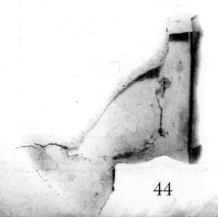

IN THE RAFTERS

(Responsibility)

BEAST YEAST

Inner Beast Release Potion
up to eight hours of nocturnal
monstrousness, ongoing
nightly transmogrifications

DO NOT CONSUME

(chocolate flavour)

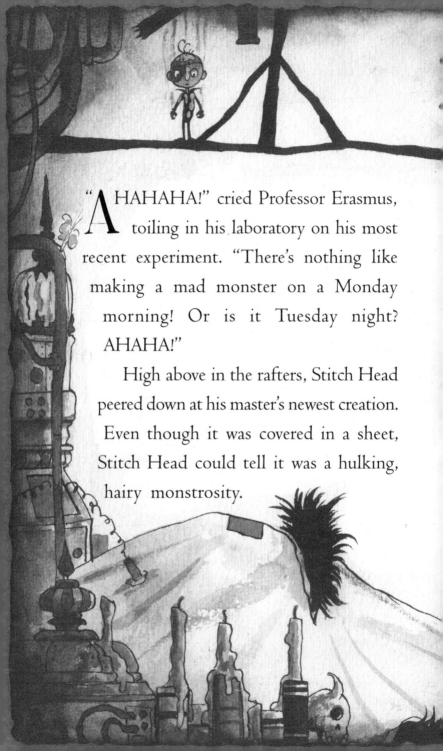

"AHAHAHA!" cried Professor Erasmus, toiling in his laboratory on his most recent experiment. "There's nothing like making a mad monster on a Monday morning! Or is it Tuesday night? AHAHA!"

High above in the rafters, Stitch Head peered down at his master's newest creation. Even though it was covered in a sheet, Stitch Head could tell it was a hulking, hairy monstrosity.

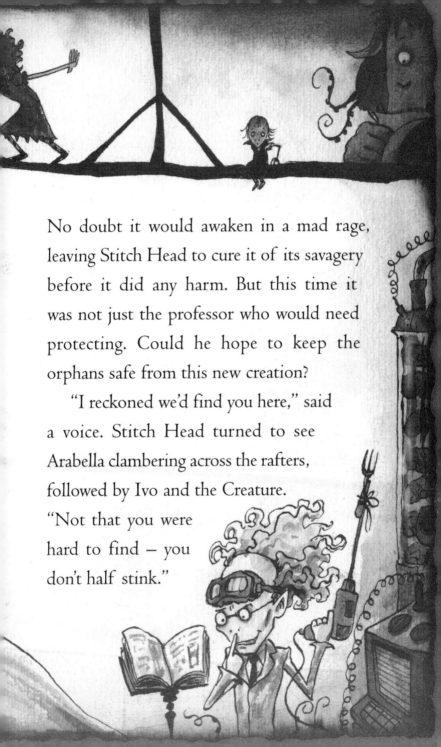

No doubt it would awaken in a mad rage, leaving Stitch Head to cure it of its savagery before it did any harm. But this time it was not just the professor who would need protecting. Could he hope to keep the orphans safe from this new creation?

"I reckoned we'd find you here," said a voice. Stitch Head turned to see Arabella clambering across the rafters, followed by Ivo and the Creature. "Not that you were hard to find — you don't half stink."

"It's the Stuff, it sticks like glue…" sighed Stitch Head.

"All part of its beguiling APPEAL," insisted the Creature.

"Are you all right, Stitch Head?" asked Ivo. "You usually do not run away from things, unless those things are trying to eat you."

"I'm sorry," replied Stitch Head. "I just needed time to think."

"I don't blame you. Ain't no fun hanging around with a bunch of ungrateful snot-necks," said Arabella, sitting on the rafter next to Stitch Head. "So, how's the prof's next monster coming along?"

"It's not finished, thank goodness," Stitch Head replied. "You see that bottle on the potion table? The small one, with the claw on it?"

"What is it?" asked Ivo, peering down at the professor's table, laden with bubbling bottles.

"That's Beast Yeast — the most powerful potion my master has ever created," Stitch Head replied gravely. "Two parts werewolf extract, one part vampire spit, three parts undiluted monstrousness ... it's guaranteed to bring out the beast in *anything*."

"Beast, y'say?" said Arabella, peering down excitedly at the bottle. "Maybe I should have a swig myself ... teach the Little Terrors a proper lesson."

"Don't even joke — I haven't managed to make a potion to counteract it yet," Stitch Head added. "Imagine if that creation got loose in the castle… Imagine if it found the orphans."

"Yeah, *imagine*," said Arabella, a look of glee in her eye. "Hopefully it'll start with that snot-eared Cuthbert."

"But Cuthbert's *right*, Arabella," said Stitch Head. "We — *I* brought the orphans here.

They're my responsibility."

"Why are you so bothered about 'em anyway?" Arabella asked. "All their grousing 'n' bellyaching… You think I ain't hungry? 'Course I am! I just don't *moan* about it, is all. I say we hand the Little Terrors over to the folk of Grubbers Nubbin and be done with it."

"But WON'T they just put them in another AWFULAGE?" asked the Creature. "What if it's even WORSE than the LAST one?"

"It can't *get* no worse than a soul-sucking spider-lady – not unless they just plain mince the kids into pies," assured Arabella. "Either way, we'll be free of them and the creations can have their castle back."

"I know, but—" began Stitch Head. "But I *promised*. I promised to keep the orphans safe … to give them a home here, in Castle Grotteskew."

"What do you mean, promised?" said Arabella. "I didn't hear you promise nothing to nobody."

"Well, not out *loud*," confessed Stitch Head. "But a promise made to yourself is still a promise."

"You and your blinkin' promises!" huffed Arabella. "You promised the professor you'd never leave him and he don't hardly even know you *exist*."

Stitch Head said nothing, but Arabella saw a look in his eyes that she'd not seen before. For once, she knew better than to argue. Instead, she flung her hands up in the air.

"Fine," she groaned. "I won't kick the Little Terrors out on to the street ... for now. We'll do it your way, Stitch Head."

"HURRAH!" cried the Creature. "Which WAY is THAT?"

"I-I don't know — I've never had to find food before," Stitch Head replied. "But I'll do whatever it takes."

"Good ... 'cause I've got a plan, and you ain't going to like it," said Arabella. "Creature, you and Ivo make yourself useful and find some way of distracting the Little Terrors from their bellies."

"I like this idea!" said Ivo. "Even though I have no idea what the idea is."

"Can I go BACK to being a CHIEF?" asked the Creature.

"Obviously *not*. Just ... get creative," said Arabella. "Stitch Head, meet me at the Great Door at midnight. You and me, we're going to pay a visit to Grubbers Nubbin."

THE SIXTH CHAPTER

GRUBBERS NUBBIN BY NIGHT
(The nightwatchman)

WANTED
Nightwatchman

For Strollin' 'n' Patrollin' in the wee small hours. Must be keen of eye and stout of constitution. Own dog and whackin' stick preferred. No prior watching at night necessary

Please note: May encounter monsters / creatures / mad things

Three hours later, the moon was a sickle of light in the ink-black sky. A thick, bone-chilling fog had settled across the land. The orphans slept, the creations hid and the castle courtyard was silent.

Almost.

"Blinkin' stinkin' key! Where'd I put it?" growled Arabella, searching her pockets. She looked up at the Great Door and gave it a kick.

"I, uh, I always keep my key in the same place, to make sure I never lose it," Stitch Head explained. He reached into his shirt and pulled out an iron key, tied to a rope around his neck. "Not that ... I mean ... it's just a suggestion..."

"I ain't lost my key – it's misplaced itself," huffed Arabella. "Now stop crowing and get this door open."

"Are you *sure* this is a good idea, Arabella?" asked Stitch Head. "I mean, *stealing* from the townsfolk? They don't need any more reason to hate us. Couldn't we find food somewhere else?"

"Where? The moon? There *ain't* nowhere else," said Arabella, slinging two large sacks over her shoulder. "Look, no one's going to know we're even there. Now, unless you have a better idea, let's get going."

Stitch Head hoped a better idea — even an equally terrible idea — would occur to him. It didn't. He sighed, slipped the key into the lock and turned it.

"Whatever it takes," he said — and pulled open the door.

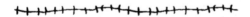

Ten minutes later, Stitch Head glanced back at the castle. Through a haze of fog, he could barely make it out atop the hill. They were almost in Grubbers Nubbin.

"Would you get a move on?" snapped Arabella, crunching down the frost-hardened hill. "You're slower than my nan, and she's been dead two weeks!"

They hurried past a sign, which read

WELCOME TO
GRUBBERS NUBBIN
(UNLESS YOU'RE A MONSTER)

…And then crept down the street. Stitch Head struggled to keep up with Arabella as she darted between two houses. He couldn't help but imagine the slumbering townsfolk tucked up inside, blissfully unaware of their plot to pilfer. It just didn't feel right.

"Arabella, I can't see a thing in all this—" Stitch Head began in a whisper, but Arabella was gone, vanished into the fog. Stitch Head's eyes darted around the icy fog. After a moment he spotted a figure in the clearing. "A-Arabella?" he whispered again.

It wasn't Arabella.

A tall human in a thick coat and flat cap was walking straight towards him. In one hand he held a baton, and with the other he restrained a large dog by a lead. Stitch Head froze as the dog sniffed the air suspiciously.

"Get in here!" hissed a voice, as Stitch Head felt an arm grab him and pull him into the alley between the houses.

"He's a *nightwatchman*," Arabella whispered. "The townsfolk must have hired him. But what have they got that's so blinkin' precious it needs— Wait, of course! Guzzlin' Day!"

"Guzzlin' Day?" repeated Stitch Head.

"The *warming winter feastival!* I forgot all about it," replied Arabella. "One day a year, folk get together and fills their guts like they ain't poor and struggling," she explained. A grin spread across her face. "The *feast*ival's in three days, and that means folk will have been stocking up. I'll bet every one of these houses is *heaving* with grub. Ripe for robbing!"

"But how do we get past the nightwatchman?" Stitch Head asked, trembling. "His *dog* is bigger than either of us..."

"Yeah and it won't be long before it picks up your stink – you still reek something awful," said Arabella, picking up a stone from the ground. "Lucky for you, dogs ain't got no sense, and most folk less than that."

With that, Arabella flung the stone as hard as she could out of the alley. It clattered to the ground on the other side of the street and Stitch Head heard a voice mutter, "Wussat?" and, "Come on, Mabel, let's 'ave a butchers…"

"It's like ol' Nan used to say, 'Days are for kicking, nights are for *sneaking*'," Arabella said with a wink, as the nightwatchman headed in the opposite direction. "Come on."

Arabella and Stitch Head hurried down a gloomy snicket until they reached the back window of a house. Arabella clambered on to a nearby dustbin and reached up to the window. She effortlessly jimmied the lock and peeked inside. By the time she looked back at Stitch Head a smile had spread across her face.

"Thank you, Guzzlin' Day!" she said excitedly. She hopped down from the bin, picked Stitch Head up and planted him on the lid. He peeked through the window to see a kitchen *bursting* with food. Loaves of bread

sat on the table, slabs of cured meat hung from the ceiling, and jars upon jars of pickles occupied the shelves.

"I used to do my best nicking around the *feast*ival. Folk have so much they don't miss a bit here and there," said Arabella with glee. Then she handed Stitch Head one of the sacks. "Remember to take a bit of everything."

"M-me?" he stuttered. "But I thought—"

"What? That I was going to do your dirty work?" Arabella replied. "Look, you want to keep the Little Terrors, you've got to take responsibility. Get in there ... I'll keep a lookout. If anything goes wrong, I'll make a sound like a one-legged pigeon."

"But ... what does a one-legged pigeon sound—?" began Stitch Head, as Arabella opened the window and pushed him inside.

THE BEAST

(Close encounters of the furred kind)

A Guzzlin' Day Ditty

You haven't ate, yer stomach's groanin'
But save yer food or you'll be moanin'
Even though the choice is harder
Keep yer grub to fill yer larder!

"Take a bit of everything," whispered Stitch Head, creeping around the kitchen. As per Arabella's instructions, he carefully helped himself to a small assortment of cakes, pies, meat, jams and pickles, so as not to make it obvious that food was missing.

"Arabella, is this enough?" he asked, lifting up the sack as he glanced back towards the window. "Do I have—"

KLANG!

A noise from outside. Stitch Head froze.

RRRRRRRR...

The growl was so deep and low it made Stitch Head's teeth ache.

"Arabella…?" he said. He tried to make the sound of a one-legged pigeon, but it just sounded like a two-legged pigeon. Suddenly a dark curved shape moved past the glass. Could it be the nightwatchman's dog? It looked bigger than any dog he'd ever seen … or any person for that matter.

He tied a knot in the top of his sack and hurried to the window. As he clambered out he saw the dustbin, lying on its side. But where was Arabella?

Stitch Head quickly pushed the sack through the window before jumping to the ground.

RRRRRRRRR…

By now Stitch Head was sure it wasn't a dog … it sounded more like a *pack* of dogs, all snarling at once. He turned and spotted the back end of something huge and dark disappear around a corner towards the main road… What was it? What if it had taken Arabella?

Stitch Head's heart beat wildly. He slung the sack over his shoulder and crept back dowm the alley. He was just about to turn into the main street when:

Rorf! Rorf!

"What is it, Mabel? What— AAH!"

Stitch Head pressed himself against the wall. The nightwatchman and his hound were close. Had they spotted Arabella?

"No!" shrieked the nightwatchman. "Away! Get away!"

"Arabella!" cried Stitch Head, leaping out from behind the wall. He was met by the horrified face of the nightwatchman – and his equally horrified dog – as they raced past him.

"Run f'your life!" the nightwatchman cried, disappearing into the fog. "It's a beast!"

RRRROOOWRR!

Stitch Head turned, slowly.

Twenty paces down the main street, he could make out a dark shape. It was as big as a horse, with dense black fur, thick broad shoulders and a mane of hair down its high, arched back. It glared at him, its eyes glowing bright white in the gloom.

"What … is … that?" Stitch Head murmured.

The beast raised itself up on to its back legs. It bared a row of huge grey fangs … and howled.

RRRROOOWRR!

Stitch Head felt his bones shake from the noise. The beast slumped back on to four legs and paced slowly towards him. Stitch Head found himself transfixed with fear and fascination. Within moments he could feel the beast's hot breath on his face. It leaned in closer, and sniffed.

BLEH!

The beast shook its head as if its nose had been stung by a wasp.

"I don't smell that bad … do I?" muttered Stitch Head.

"Lawks a mussy! A monster!" came a sudden cry. The townsfolk had been woken by the beast's howls. They spilled out into the street, clad in nightgowns and carrying candles. The beast gnashed its jaws and let out an almighty

RRRROOOWRR!

…Before leaping down a side street and vanishing into the gloom.

"Wait! Come back! Who … who are you?" asked Stitch Head. He dropped his sack of food, and raced after the beast, hurrying between the legs of the townsfolk as they ran about in panic.

"The mad professor has sent another monster to our town!"

"I warned you it'd happen again!"

"I warned you first!"

"I warned you *ages* ago."

"I warned you when you wasn't even 'ere."

"Where was I?"

"Off visiting your auntie Maude in Drubbers Dollop."

"So I was. Good old Auntie Maude – she's got the loveliest little bungalow on the coast. Have you ever been to Drubbers Dollop?"

"I ain't, I confess."

"Why, it's charmin'! The blooms in spring really are the most—"

"Would you two shut up and fetch the torches!"

"And the pitchforks!"

"Oh yes, don't forget the pitchforks!"

The townsfolk's chatter had already faded as Stitch Head pursued the beast's great claw prints down the alley. He raced after it, with absolutely no plan of action should he catch up with it. Then he spotted something in the shifting fog.

The door to one of the houses had been smashed open.

Stitch Head crept inside, clambering over the splintered wood and followed the trail of destruction into the kitchen.

RRRRRRRR...

In the gloom, he could just make out the back end of the beast – the sound of its great jaws crunching through a larder full of food. Stitch Head edged gingerly towards it, took a deep shuddering breath and whispered, "H-hello?"

RAARR!

The beast reared up with shock, smacking its head on the ceiling. Before Stitch Head could even gasp, it had backed out of the larder and spun around to face him. He saw the beast's right claw rushing towards his head, and a moment later felt himself flying through the air. He smashed hard into a wall and fell limply to the ground.

With his head spinning, Stitch Head watched the beast loom over him. His last thought was of Arabella, before he slipped into unconsciousness.

THE MORNING AFTER THE NIGHTMARE BEFORE
(Getting out of Grubbers Nubbin)

MAD MUSING No. 765

"Monstrous is as madness does."

From *The Occasionally Scientific Writings of Professor Erasmus Erasmus*

"Stitch Head, wake up!"

Stitch Head opened his eyes to see Arabella looming over him. He could barely move. A painful chill gnawed at his fingers and toes. He could hear the sound of panicked voices nearby ... *human* voices.

"Wuh...? What's happening?" he said. He sat up and hit his head on the bottom of a table. He was still in the kitchen of the house, but morning light streamed through the window and stung his eyes. "What happened to you?"

"I dunno! Don't hardly remember a thing," said Arabella. "I was keeping a lookout by the window, then the next thing I know I wake up inside a dustbin with a bump on my noggin and half frozen t'death!"

"Are you all right?" said Stitch Head.

"Never mind about that," she said, rubbing the back of her head. "There's townsfolk everywhere, fretting about some beast. They're saying it attacked the town last night ... ate half the food for Guzzlin' Day!"

"I *saw* it ... I saw the beast!" said Stitch Head. "It was as big as the Creature, with teeth and claws and hair and eyes and ... monstrousness. *Lots* of monstrousness."

"Speaking of which, the townsfolk ain't going to take kindly to finding you here," said Arabella. "We should make ourselves scarce."

She pulled Stitch Head to his feet and hurried out of the house. As they left, she grabbed a tea towel and threw it over his head. Stitch Head kept his head low, but he could hear the humans' panicked cries and see their feet as they raced about. He dared to lift the tea towel a little, and glanced back to witness the beast's devastation. Doors and windows were smashed to pieces, and the wreckage was strewn over the street.

"It must have been one of the creations…" he whispered.

"But that ain't possible, is it?" replied Arabella, as they sped out of town. "Ain't none of the prof's creations monstrous enough to do this – they can't even handle the Little Terrors."

"But where could it come from but the castle?" said Stitch Head. "There's only one explanation: one of our monsters is actually *monstrous*."

COUNTING CREATIONS

(The wisdom of Ivo)

Name	Features to distinguish (for comparison to beast)	Approximation of Monstrous Intent, recorded as a percentage (%)	Knowledge of (or likeness to) The Beast of Grubbers Nubbin?
Irving	Free-floating, exposed brain, excellent teeth	1.2	NO
Myrtle	Four arms, three legs, two heads, no body	1.0	NO
Wilfred	Six clawed hands (all trimmed), hair (shaven)	0.6	NO
Columbus	Skull for face, wheels for feet	0.02	NO

Stitch Head and Arabella hurried back to the castle. They unlocked the Great Door and pushed it open, to be met by Cuthbert and an assemblage of orphans.

"Did you bring us breakfast? Oh, tell us you did!" cried Cuthbert loudly. "How weak I feel! I'm not sure I'll last another day…"

"Shut it, you meat pie, you'll outlast the lot of us!" replied Arabella. "Anyway, we ain't got time to feed your fat face, we've got a beast to worry about!"

"A b-b-beast?" whimpered Squit.

"Calm down, Squit – we have nothing to fear from B-E-E-S-T-S," huffed Cuthbert. "This whole castle is *full* of them and they're too scared to come out. There's nothing monstrous about any of them."

"I hope you're right…" Stitch Head whispered to himself.

Stitch Head and Arabella spent all day searching the castle for Professor Erasmus's creations. Stitch Head was convinced that one of them *had* to at least know the beast — if they weren't the beast themselves.

"Glowing eyes and gnashing teeth, you say? Sounds a bit like my second wife," said Septimus, a glow-in-the-gloom skeleton creature. "Except she's as bald as you, my stitched-together friend!"

"Covered in black fur? Why, that would describe half my bridge club," declared Dorothea, a flying eyeball. "Of course none of them are even halfway huge. In fact Clementine has actually lost a few pounds, or so she *claims…*"

"I've certainly not been bothered by any beast, they can stay as long as they wish," said Bertram, a dog made of cats. "The orphans, on the other hand, make *such* a racket… I don't suppose they're leaving any time soon?"

By nightfall Stitch Head had accounted for all three hundred and thirteen of Professor Erasmus's creations … and not one of them was even slightly beastly.

"So if the beast ain't from the castle, where did it come from?" huffed Arabella, as they made their way through dark corridors. "You sure it wasn't just a blinkin' big dog?"

"I'm sure – that thing had 'mad science' written all over it," replied Stitch Head. "I just can't believe no one's even seen it. How could anything so … so beastly go unnoticed for—"

KRUNG!

KRUNNG!

KRUNNNNG!

"*Now* what?" groaned Arabella, as the strange sound echoed around the castle. "One of them Little Terrors, no doubt!"

"Or the beast," added Stitch Head. "Come on!"

They raced down the corridor until they reached the familiar north wing of the castle. The noise getting louder and louder as they approached...

"The Creature's room!" cried Stitch Head. "It's coming from inside the—"

"Stop!" The tiny figure of Ivo leaped out from behind a pillar, blocking their path. "You cannot go in! We are working hard on orphan distraction idea. Creature is very private about creative process! Also, it has not finished making unicycle yet."

"*Unicycle?*" repeated Stitch Head, suspiciously. "What's going on? What are you two planning?"

"It is secret," replied Ivo. He reached into his ragged cloak, and with an impressive flourish, pulled out a candle, already lit and flaming. "Just wait … we give the orphans something *better* than food."

"Sounds like a disaster waiting to happen," chuckled Arabella. "I can't wait."

"Is exciting! You will see!" Ivo declared. "So, have you solved mystery of who is beast?"

"We've spoken to every creation in the castle, and no one's ever even seen it," sighed Stitch Head. "What if it's still out there? If the beast keeps attacking Grubbers Nubbin, the townsfolk will come to the castle…"

"Let 'em come!" said Arabella, her fists clenched.

"More is merrier! I like humans!" added Ivo. "I like Angry Girl because she is loud and strange and kicks things for no reason!"

"I should think so, too," Arabella said with a grin.

"But humans are like candlelight," Ivo added, peering at the flame. "One candle is good, but many candles are too bright ... too hot. The light make all the shadows disappear. When humans goes to a place, they makes that place a human place."

"We just need to find the beast. As long as we can find the beast everything will be OK," said Stitch Head unconvincingly, his sense of dread deepening. "But I don't even know where to look. For once it might not even have come from the ... professor's ... laboratory..."

Stitch Head's eyes grew wide. He turned to Arabella.

"The laboratory!" they cried together. "There's one creation left!"

They raced away with such speed that it blew out Ivo's candle. Ivo stood in the darkness for a long moment.

"It was something I said?"

IN SEARCH OF THE BEAST

(One of our potions is missing)

MAD MUSING NO. 432

"Lose your mind, not your potion."

From *The Occasionally Scientific Writings of Professor Erasmus Erasmus*

Within minutes, Stitch Head and Arabella were back in the rafters above the castle laboratory.

"Where is it? It's gone!" cried the professor, rushing from one end of the laboratory to the other.

"Hear that? We were *right*, Stitch Head," said Arabella, following him to the middle of the rafter. "The prof's brought his new monster to almost-life already, and it's gone and done a runner to Grubbers Nubbin!"

"Why didn't I think of it before?" replied Stitch Head, peering down over the rafter. "And *how* did I not notice my master's creation was ready ahead of— Wait!"

"What?" asked Arabella.

Stitch Head pointed to the creating table. "It can't be," he blurted. "It's *still there*."

Sure enough, the professor's newest

creation lay half-finished and lifeless on the table, a hairy leg hanging out from under the sheet. Stitch Head breathed a sigh of relief.

"Gone! Lost! Where is it?" the professor shrieked, searching in vain.

"Hang on a sec," Arabella began, peering down at the professor. "If that old fungus ain't lost his creation, what *has* he lost? Apart from his mind..."

Stitch Head squinted, glancing around the laboratory. He'd become an expert at memorizing the many and varied "ingredients" that populated the shelves, desks and cabinets — it was in his best interests to know what was going into his master's mad experiments. After a moment, his stare fixed upon the professor's potion table.

"Wait ... there's a bottle missing. It's— Oh *no*," he said. "The Beast Yeast! It's *gone.*"

"And?" shrugged Arabella. "That daft old lizard's a hundred years old and a pie short of a picnic. He'll just have lost it."

"The professor is insane ... but he's not absent-minded," Stitch Head explained. "He's never lost a potion, not in all the time I've been creating antidotes for them. Someone must have *taken* it. But who?"

"The Little Terrors, of course!" snarled Arabella. "Bound to be one of them thievin' grubs. They don't like nothin' more than doing something they ain't meant to be doing."

"But would they really steal from…?" began Stitch Head, then remembered he himself had tried to steal from Grubbers Nubbin only last night. Arabella was right, she had to be … and Stitch Head couldn't risk anyone jeopardizing his master's experiments.

"OK, first we have to stop the orphans getting in here and taking anything else," he concluded. "Then we find the missing potion, return it to the professor, get food for the orphans, and find the beast of—"

"Hang on a tic – I ain't doing nothin' before I get some shut eye," said Arabella, stifling a yawn. "I ain't like you monsters, much as I'd like to be – I need a good night's sleep."

"Of course! Sorry … you go to bed. I'll come and get you in the morning," replied Stitch Head. With that, Arabella let out such a massive yawn that even Stitch Head felt sleepy.

"Fair enough," she said. "Just stay out of trouble 'til sunrise."

"I'll try," replied Stitch Head.

But little did he know, trouble was already here.

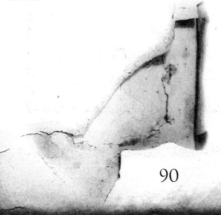

THE FIGURE IN THE FOG
(Return to Grubbers Nubbin)

MAD MUSING NO. 622

"An ocean of potion will set
things in motion."

From *The Occasionally Scientific
Writings of Professor Erasmus Erasmus*

Night and thick fog had fallen over Grotteskew. With Arabella and the rest of the orphans sleeping and the castle's creations hiding in distant corners, the castle was unnervingly silent.

Stitch Head had spent more than an hour carefully, quietly piling furniture in front of the laboratory door. His makeshift barricade would not be enough to keep out a determined thief, but there was no way anyone could get past without causing a racket. As Stitch Head heaped chair upon table upon desk, he felt as if questions, too, were piling up in front of him. Who had stolen the potion and why? Could they have known what they were taking? Could there be some connection to the Beast of Grubbers Nubbin? Where was the beast now? Where had it come from? And how could it just disappear in the middle of—

CLUNK.

The noise was distant but familiar — *a key turning in the Great Door.*

Stitch Head abandoned his barricade and raced towards the courtyard. It had to be Arabella — she must have found her lost key. But what was she doing up, and why was she unlocking the castle door?

Stitch Head rounded the corner to see the door open and ajar. He hurried across the courtyard and rushed through the doorway out into the night. As he squinted in the haze, he spotted something — a small figure, hurrying down the hill. The fog was so thick that Stitch Head couldn't make out who it was, but it was human.

A human child.

"Arabella…?" Stitch Head began in a whisper, but he couldn't be sure it was her.

As the figure disappeared into the fog, he locked the door behind him, and raced down the hill.

Stitch Head pursued the figure all the way to the outskirts of town. The street lamps in the town were still lit, and Stitch Head could see the doors to the houses had been nailed shut, and the windows boarded up with planks of wood.

That's going to make it a lot harder to get food, thought Stitch Head. *If there's any left…*

The figure suddenly stopped in its tracks, not thirty paces from the town. It leaned weakly against a tree, as if suddenly faint. Stitch Head edged towards it, eager to confirm it was Arabella. But as he got closer, the figure began to shiver … then shake … then *grow*.

"What…?" uttered Stitch Head. He saw the figure contort and change shape. He heard the crunch of shifting bone and the stretching of muscle. The figure doubled … tripled … quadrupled its size, and great clumps of dark hair sprouted from its body.

In a matter of seconds, where once was a human child, stood

THE BEAST.

"It can't be … the Beast Yeast!" said Stitch Head. He kicked himself for not making the connection earlier. The thief didn't just steal the Beast Yeast … they *drank* it.

RRURR...

With its terrible transformation complete, the beast fell on to all fours and began loping towards town.

"Wait, stop!" Without thinking, Stitch Head sprinted after the beast as fast as he could, his body still bruised from their last encounter. The fog was so thick he momentarily lost sight of it … until he saw its eyes burning white in the gloom.

The beast was right in front of him.

RRR...

"A-Arabella…?" he whispered. "Is that you?"

The beast cocked its head to one side, its hot breath puffing out from between grey teeth. For a moment, it seemed to recognize Stitch Head. It leaned in and gave him a sniff.

BLEH!

The beast groaned, and quickly turned to go.

"Wait! Don't go back to town, please!" cried Stitch Head, racing after it. He darted in front of the beast, desperately trying to block its path. The beast stepped left and right, its white eyes burned with monstrous rage, but Stitch Head leaped in front of it again and again.

"P-please, stop … I can cure you," he whimpered. "I can—"

RRAARGH!

The beast roared, swatting Stitch Head with a great claw. Stitch Head crashed with a THOMP into a nearby tree. He squealed in pain and slumped to the ground. His head was spinning as he saw the beast rise up on its hind legs and dig its claws into the tree. With a roar, it wrenched it out of the ground and raised the tree over its head.

RRRRRRRR!

"Uh-oh..." Stitch Head muttered.

KRUMP.

ONE HUNDRED SUSPECTS

(Who drank the potion?)

Grubbers Nubbin
Notice Board

Beast has eaten all pies

Please bake more pies

"Smash your nose into— Uh?"

Arabella awoke and sat bolt upright, squinting at the morning light coming through her window. It took her a moment to remember she was in her bedroom in the castle.

Stitch Head was standing at the foot of her bed, staring back at her.

"Blimey! What happened to you?" she squealed. Stitch Head was in a worse state

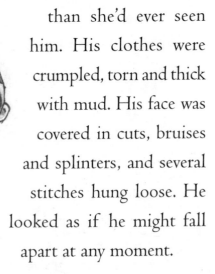

than she'd ever seen him. His clothes were crumpled, torn and thick with mud. His face was covered in cuts, bruises and splinters, and several stitches hung loose. He looked as if he might fall apart at any moment.

100

"The beast dropped a tree on top of me … took me all night to dig myself free…" muttered Stitch Head deliriously. "But that's not important."

"The beast did this to you?" said Arabella. "I'll kick its head off!"

Stitch Head peered at her, more suspicious than ever. He'd had all night to think – and dig – and had spent the time trying to solve the mystery of the beast, to piece together the clues in his mind…

Arabella knew about the Beast Yeast's effects. I explained them to her while we sat in the rafters above the laboratory.

Arabella talked about drinking the potion, to "teach the Little Terrors a Lesson".

That first night in Grubbers Nubbin, Arabella suddenly vanished from the alley. Moments later, the beast appeared.

When the beast was looking for food, it struck its head on the ceiling of the larder. Hours later, when Arabella found me, she complained of a bump on her own head, and had no memory of the night.

The Great Door was unlocked — and Arabella had the only other key.

Stitch Head could not help but think the unthinkable. What if Arabella had taken the Beast Yeast? What if *she* was the Beast of Grubbers Nubbin?

"Arabella ... did you leave the castle last night?" he asked grimly.

"Leave the castle?" Arabella replied. "What, and go for an ice-cold stroll in the pitch dark?"

"Someone unlocked the Great Door," Stitch Head explained, examining her for a response. "A human."

"Don't look at me, I ain't even found my

key yet," said Arabella with a yawn. "It was probably one of the Little Terrors you saw, sneaking about like a rat."

"The orphans...?" replied Stitch Head. "But ... but how would they have opened the door?"

"Probably picked the lock," replied Arabella. "Half of them orphans have been breakin' and enterin' all their lives. Bunch of burglarizing bandits..."

Stitch Head hadn't even considered it. Could one of the orphans have *picked the lock* to the Great Door? It seemed impossible – the door was virtually impenetrable! And how could they know about the Beast Yeast? It didn't quite add up ... but if there was even a slim chance Arabella was right, then that meant he had *one hundred* possible suspects. A hundred suspects he barely even knew.

"What's this all about, Stitch Head?" asked Arabella. Stitch Head suddenly felt guilty and foolish for doubting her, when they were so many possibilities he hadn't even considered. How *could* she be the beast? After all, she was his friend – and the only human he'd ever trusted.

He took a deep breath, and put his doubts behind him.

"I'll explain on the way," he replied. "We have to gather the orphans."

Ten minutes later, Stitch Head and Arabella stood at the end of the dining hall, the sound of the dinner bell echoing through the castle. Within moments, the children stampeded into the room.

"Ninety-eight … ninety-nine … one

hundred," said Stitch Head, counting them in. "They're all here. Every one of them."

"Potion-swilling, monster-turning-into Little Terrors! I should have guessed one of them is your beast!" Arabella growled, her clenched fists shaking as the orphans took their seats. "I should have  kicked 'em out when I had the chance."

"Arabella, we have to be ... *delicate* about this," said Stitch Head. "If one of them is the beast, they'll have returned to human form with the daylight. We have to find out who it is without causing a *panic*."

"Leave it to me," Arabella snarled. She clambered up on top of the table and stamped her feet. "Oi! Shut your faces or I'll fill 'em with my boot!"

"Please tell us you didn't summon us here so you could throw insults at us again, mad thing," groaned Cuthbert, his voice even louder than Arabella's. He grabbed Squit by his scrawny arm and held it up. "Look at us! We're wasting away! We need food!"

The other children quickly echoed the sentiment in loud, hungry groans.

"There ain't no food!" Arabella shouted. "And there ain't going to *be* none, since one of you keeps turning into a beast and nicking all the grub we was fixing to nick for you in the first place!"

"Not *exactly* what I meant by delicate…" Stitch Head sighed.

"So in a castle filled with monsters, you're saying one of *us* is a beast?" scoffed Cuthbert.

"Yeah! And I reckon if anyone's scoffing the townsfolk's grub, it's you, you great tub o' butter!" Arabella growled, rolling up her sleeves.

"Or perhaps it's *you*, mad thing," Cuthbert sneered. "Perhaps this was your plan all along – to frame us poor orphans for a crime we didn't commit!"

"That's it! I've had enough of you – and your gob!" shouted Arabella, stamping towards Cuthbert. "I'm going to kick your teeth into next week!"

"Orphans, protect me! I am your spokesperson!" cried Cuthbert. Squit stepped into Arabella's path but she kicked him in the shin and grabbed him in a headlock.

"My n-n-n-neck…!" Squit whimpered, fumbling feebly at Arabella's dress as she dragged him across the floor. She waded into the crowd, kicking chairs and children, shoving the orphans out of the dining hall like a savage dog herding sheep.

"Go on, get out, the lot of you!" she cried, tossing Squit into the crowd of children like a bowling ball. "Shove off out of it! See how the real world likes you!"

"Arabella, wait!" Stitch Head began. "This isn't—"

BOOOM!

The door at the other end of the room burst open.

"Creature...?" muttered Stitch Head. The Creature was barely recognizable as it strode into the room. Its face was painted bright white, with a thick covering of red lipstick around its mouth. Its hair was striped with different colours and it wore a white costume with a wide ruff collar. Ivo hurried in behind him, with a red dot painted on his face where his nose should be and dragging a heavily laden sack behind him.

"Ladies and GENTLESMELLS, we're BACK!" the Creature cried. "And we're going to make you WET your PANTS!"

"With laughter!" added Ivo. "Hopefully."

CLOWNING AROUND
(That's enter-trainment)

MAD MUSING NO. 224

"If madness be the food of science,
serve me a double helping."

From *The Occasionally Scientific
Writings of Professor Erasmus Erasmus*

"That's what the Creature was doing all this time? Turning itself into a *clown*?" said Arabella, as the Creature skipped into the room.

"EXACTLY! And what BETTER way to distract the awfuls than with ENTER-TRAINMENT?" explained the Creature.

"Uh-oh," muttered Stitch Head.

"I feel a SONG coming on … a DITTY so DROLL you'll SOIL yourselves!" the Creature continued. "PREPARE to FORGET your HUNGER!"

With that the Creature broke into tuneless song, with Ivo dancing an enthusiastic jig beside it.

BREAD and EGGS and BACON and a
LANCASHIRE hot POT,
CAKES and BUNS and FRUIT and
ALE are things you HAVEN'T got!
APPLE pie and PUDDING, all washed
DOWN with ginger BEER,
SAUSAGE and POTATOES are
unlikely to appear!
TREACLE TART with CUSTARD or a
TASTY hot cross BUN,
The CHANCES you will eat 'em are
a MILLION to one!
'Cause you are HUNGRY! HUNGRY!
All you want is FOOD!
You're DESPERATE to
fill your guts
IS what we must CONCLUDE
Oh, you are HUNGRY! HUNGRY!
All you want's a MEAL
You're desperate to EAT something
We DON'T know how you feel!

"SING along!" cried the Creature, gleefully. "Even though you DON'T know the WORDS!"

You're SCRAPING by on ANTS and
FLIES, whatever you can find,
You LITERALLY would KILL your
friend for MOULDY bacon rind
You're eating SCABS from off your
KNEES, it's NOT much of a TREAT
But HERE'S a little DITTY that
is GOOD enough to eat!
OH, you are HUNGRY! HUNGRY!
All you want is FOOD!
You're DESPERATE to fill your guts
That's what we must
CONCLUUUUUUUUUDE!

The Creature and Ivo struck a showy pose, their arms out wide, broad grins across their faces.

There was a long silence.

Then the rumble of a stomach.

Then a single cough.

Then:

"You sloppy muck-heads!" howled Arabella. "You're meant to be making us – I mean *them* – forget their hunger, not remind 'em of it!" She pointed at the children, clutching their aching bellies.

"Don't WORRY, we're just getting STARTED! Ivo, PULL my TOGGLE of HILARITY!" cried the Creature.

Ivo obediently yanked on a rope hanging from the Creature's belt. Its trousers fell to the floor to reveal a pair of spotty bloomers.

"See how the underwear amuses!" declared Ivo. Stitch Head leaped out of the way as the Creature broke into a forward roll, crashing into a chair and then colliding with the table.

"Now watch THIS! Ivo, hand me the BLADES of MERRIMENT!" the Creature continued, pulling up its trousers as it leaped to its feet.

"*Blades?*" blurted Stitch Head. Ivo drew a sharp knife out of the bag and then flung it at the Creature! The knife flew past its ear and landed with a SHUNK in the wall.

"KEEP 'em COMING!" cried the Creature, tugging the knife out. "It DOESN'T count as JUGGLING until I've got at least THREE!

"But ... wait!" cried Stitch Head, as Ivo threw more knives at the Creature. One landed with a THUD-D-D in the table. Another bounced off a wall and whooshed past Arabella's ear, while a third landed with a THOP ... in the Creature's foot.

"AAH!" cried the Creature.

"Aaah!" screamed the orphans.

"Aaaaah!" added Ivo. "Was accident!"

"This actually *is* pretty entertaining," chuckled Arabella.

"There are no – OW – accidents in ENTER-TRAINMENT," the Creature said, gingerly pulling out the knife. "Just – OOWW – opportunities for HILARITY!"

"Hilaritunities!" cried Ivo.

"It's WORKING ... they're LOVING it!" concluded the Creature. "Time to bring out the BIG guns ... the FLAMING UNICYCLE!"

"The *what?*" Stitch Head shrieked, as Ivo dragged out a tiny, single-wheeled cycle out of the bag. The Creature clambered on to it and immediately started to pedal furiously, back and forth. Ivo then produced a lit candle from inside his coat – and held it to the wheel.

"Just – YOOW – like in REHEARSAL!" the Creature yelped, as the flames spat upwards, igniting the seat of his trousers. It zoomed backwards and forwards, desperately trying to blow out the fire.

"Stop this!" Stitch Head cried. "Stop before—"

It was then Stitch Head heard something he hadn't heard in days – the sound of *laughter*. What started out as a giggle quickly progressed to a chuckle, and ended up as a full-blown guffaw. The Creature was right – it *was* working. The children were laughing!

"They like it. They actually like it…" Stitch Head whispered excitedly. "It's *perfect*. Creature, Ivo, don't stop! I mean, unless you need to put the flames out…"

"No PROBLEM!" cried the Creature. "I think I was MADE to be an ENTER-TRAINER! I've finally found my CALLING…"

Stitch Head grabbed Arabella by the arm and dragged her towards the door.

"Oi! Where we going?" she said. "I ain't finished kicking the Little Terrors out of the castle!"

"I've got a better idea," replied Stitch Head. "The Creature just bought us some time…"

"Time? For what?" Arabella asked, with a hint of disappointment.

"A *cure*," Stitch Head said. "One of the

orphans is going to *change* at nightfall. If the Creature can keep them happy here, then I can work on creating a potion to cure the beast. I have 'til the end of the day."

"*Or* we could just—" began Arabella, but Stitch Head was already speeding out of the room. She watched the children howl with laughter as the Creature accidentally set fire to its tail.

"Oi, Stitch Head! Wait for me!" she cried, and raced after him.

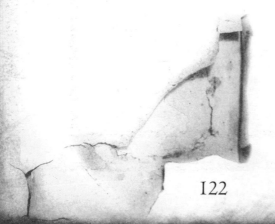

THE BOTTLE

(Working on a cure)

MAD MUSING NO. 584

"Never trust anyone you haven't made yourself."

From *The Occasionally Scientific Writings of Professor Erasmus Erasmus*

"More Wolf-Away potion, maybe? Or Blood Blank anti-vampire vial?" mused Stitch Head. He and Arabella had lost track of time as they toiled in the dungeon, looking for a cure for Professor Erasmus's Beast Yeast. "No wait! A drop of Monstrousness Moderating Mixture! Arabella, would you hand me that green bottle? Be careful, it's volatile…"

"I know how it feels," grumbled Arabella, handing him the vial.

"This will work, you'll see – no more beast, no more problems, no more surprises," Stitch Head assured her. He uncorked the bottle and poured a drop of the green liquid into an already-bubbling mixture.

KROOOMSH!

Stitch Head's mixture exploded, sending him and Arabella flying backwards across the dungeon.

"Urf!"

"Oof!"

KLINK!

Something fell out of Arabella's pocket and on to the floor. It rolled along the ground and into Stitch Head's foot.

"Arabella, are you all right?" coughed Stitch Head. "Sorry, the Monstrousness Moderating Mixture must have reacted with the Crazed Creature Curative. But we're close, I know it! A little more— Huh?"

He glanced down. At his feet was a tiny, empty bottle, with a claw painted on the front. Stitch Head felt his blood run cold.

"The Beast Yeast…?" he blurted. He stared at Arabella as she got to her feet. "How … how did you get this?"

"I ain't never seen that before in my life," replied Arabella defensively. "I mean, obviously I've seen it in the prof's lab the other day, but I ain't got a clue how it got in my pocket."

Stitch Head said nothing. He just stared at her.

"What you gawping at?" asked Arabella. "That *ain't* mine."

"In the rafters … I told you about the potion," muttered Stitch Head. "No one else knew what it was. Just me, Ivo, the Creature … and you."

"Yeah, so?" snapped Arabella.

The truth has been staring me in the stitches, thought Stitch Head. *I just didn't want to believe it!*

"'Maybe I should have a swig myself'," you said," Stitch Head continued. "'Teach the Little Terrors a proper lesson.'"

"I swear, Stitch Head, you had better not be thinking of accusing me of what I think you're thinking of accusing me," Arabella growled. "I did not drink that potion!"

"I . . . I wouldn't blame you," replied Stitch Head, backing away. "I know how much you want the orphans out of the castle. You knew that if you could enrage the townsfolk . . . if you could get them to come to the castle, they might take the orphans away."

"That's a pile of stinkin' knickers!" Arabella howled. "Yeah, I want them orphans gone, but not enough to turn myself into a monster! What's got into you? Don't you believe me?"

"I. . . " muttered Stitch Head, trying to think of an answer. But he already found himself edging towards the dungeon door.

"Where you going? Don't you dare. Don't you dare do what I think you're going to do…!" Arabella roared.

But he did. Stitch Head raced out of the dungeon, slammed the door shut and slid the bolt across the door.

"Oi! Lemme out! I ain't no beast!" roared Arabella from inside. She tried to pull open the door, before banging on it with her fists. "Stitch Head!"

"I'm sorry, Arabella … but I can't," he replied, not quite able to believe what he'd done. "I'll find a way to cure you, I *promise!*"

"I don't need curing! Open this door!" Arabella howled. Her cries were still ringing out as Stitch Head rushed up the stairs and away.

COPING WITH CHANGE

(What to do when your best friend turns out to be a beast)

Grubbers Nubbin Notice Board

HAVE YOU SEEN THIS MONSTER?

Wanted in connection with scarin', gluttony and monstrousness most unholy. Please report any sightings at the town hall

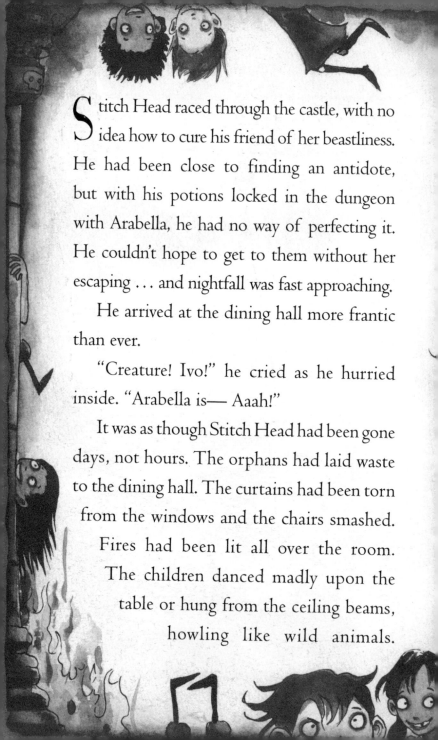

Stitch Head raced through the castle, with no idea how to cure his friend of her beastliness. He had been close to finding an antidote, but with his potions locked in the dungeon with Arabella, he had no way of perfecting it. He couldn't hope to get to them without her escaping ... and nightfall was fast approaching.

He arrived at the dining hall more frantic than ever.

"Creature! Ivo!" he cried as he hurried inside. "Arabella is— Aaah!"

It was as though Stitch Head had been gone days, not hours. The orphans had laid waste to the dining hall. The curtains had been torn from the windows and the chairs smashed. Fires had been lit all over the room. The children danced madly upon the table or hung from the ceiling beams, howling like wild animals.

Several were stacked on the Creature's unicycle, racing madly around the room. Yet more duelled with chair legs. Fuelled by the Creature's preposterous performance and their own hunger-induced delirium, they had completely lost their senses. It was chaos.

"Stitch Head! Come and JOIN the FUN!" came a cry. At the far end of the room, tied up to a chair with the curtain cord was the Creature.

"What ... what happened here?" asked Stitch Head, rushing over.

"Isn't this GREAT? After my FIFTY-EIGHTH song, the awfuls decided they'd LIKE to have a GO at enter-training THEMSELVES," said the Creature, happily.

"Please to tell me when it is over," squeaked a voice, as Ivo emerged from beneath the singed remains of the Creature's clown costume. "Orphans creativity is *terrifying*."

"Creativity? *How* is this creative?" Stitch Head blurted, surveying the destruction as he helped Ivo to the ground.

"ART is SUBJECTIVE," noted the Creature. "ANYWAY, it would be

IRRESPONSIBLE to try and SUPPRESS their IMAGINATION…"

"Never mind about— Look! We have a bigger problem!" said Stitch Head. "Arabella is the *Beast of Grubbers Nubbin.*"

"She IS? That's GREAT!" cried the Creature. "No, WAIT, that's TERRIBLE."

"When night falls, she's going to transform into the beast again," Stitch Head continued, hurriedly untying the Creature. "And I've locked her in the dungeon, along with any chance of curing her!"

"Did I hear you correctly?" said a familar voice. Cuthbert emerged from the chaos wearing the Creature's huge collar like a makeshift crown. Squit scurried behind him, holding the back of his blazer as if it was a royal train. "Have you *finally* done the decent thing and locked that dreadful Arabella away?"

he continued. "Does this mean you are now free to fetch us some food? Oh, sweet mercy, say it is so!"

"H-h-hungry..." muttered Squit, lurking in Cuthbert's shadow.

"I … I…" Stitch Head began.

"AWFULS of Grotteskew!" boomed the Creature, his arms held high. "Today, you have FED upon the rich FEAST of enter-trainment … but I KNOW you are still HUNGRY. Well, do not FEAR! TOMORROW you will have more food than you can POSSIBLY eat! A FEAST! And THAT'S a PROMISE!"

"Hooray!" cried a gleeful Ivo.

"Creature, what are you—?" began Stitch Head in disbelief. "We don't *have* any food to give them!"

"That's a good POINT," replied the Creature. "But now Arabella's LOCKED up, there's NO more BEAST to stop you STEALING the FOOD the beast stole that YOU were supposed to be STEALING in the FIRST place, RIGHT?"

Stitch Head glanced out of the window

and saw the sun still hanging in the sky. The Creature was actually right – after dark he could go to Grubbers Nubbin without having to worry about the beast.

But there was still an hour of daylight left – time enough to work on a cure for Arabella.

All he needed were his potions.

THE LIBRARY

(Just like a Dingle Dangle)

MAD MUSING NO. 337

"Read to feed."

From *The Occasionally Scientific Writings of Professor Erasmus Erasmus*

Having collected up the rest of the curtain cords, Stitch Head, the Creature and Ivo left the dining hall and made their way through the castle.

"So what is plan? We will do anything to help Angry Girl," said Ivo.

"In the mood Arabella's in, I think the best plan is to keep our distance," said Stitch Head. "Or at least *look* like we are…"

A few murky corridors later, they arrived in a large library. It was filled with shelf after shelf of books. Most had not been read until a week ago (since Professor Erasmus only read books about mad science). Now the books were open, read and strewn about by the orphans.

"STORY TELLERING! What a GREAT idea," cried the Creature. "I think I was MADE to be a—"

"Shhh … she'll *hear* us," said Stitch Head. As the Creature scratched its chin in confusion, Stitch Head crept over to a large, dusty armchair in one corner of the room. With all his strength he pushed it aside, and then pulled back the rug beneath.

There was a hole in the floor, not much bigger than a dustbin lid, descending into darkness.

"What is it?" said Ivo, peering into the hole. "Apart from obvious health hazard."

"It's a *listening trumpet*," whispered Stitch Head. "I made them years ago so I could, well, listen ... so I could keep the professor safe. There are dozens of them all over the castle. And every one of them—"

"Leads BACK to the DUNGEON!" the Creature cried.

"Shhh!" said Stitch Head again, pressing his finger to his lips.

"I like this plan," whispered Ivo. "Also, what is plan?"

"If I'm going to create a cure, I'll need my potions," Stitch Head replied. "But we can't risk Arabella escaping, so our only chance is to take them without her noticing." He quickly knotted the curtain cords together, until they formed a single long rope. "The trumpet should be big enough for me to fit through – and it's the most direct route to the dungeon. A long, sharp drop, all the way to the bottom. All you need to do is lower me down."

"JUST like a DINGLE DANGLE!" said the Creature excitedly. Stitch Head shuddered as he remembered the Creature's favourite "game", which involved flinging Stitch Head from a great height with a rope tied to his ankle. He didn't care to repeat the experience … but Arabella's humanity was at stake.

"Yes, just like a Dingle Dangle," Stitch Head sighed, securing one end of the rope around his waist. He perched over the hole and took a deep breath. "I'll tug on the rope – once for more slack, twice to come back up. OK?"

"GOT it! Happy LANDINGS!" cried the Creature — and shoved Stitch Head into the hole.

"I am not expert at dingle or dangle," said Ivo, scratching his head. "But do we not need to hold other end of rope?"

DOWN THE TRUMPET HOLE

(Retrieving the potions)

Grubbers Nubbin Notice Board

Tomorrow is Guzzlin' Day, our Warmin' Winter Feastival! Come one, come all!

Note: Guzzlin' Day subject to cancellation due to persistent beastliness.

cancellation may be cancelled without notice. Please check notice board.

Stitch Head plummeted at full speed down the trumpet hole. He couldn't risk Arabella hearing him – even trying to slow his descent would send echoes through the dungeon ... although he was pretty sure she'd see *and* hear him when he shot out of the other end and splatted on to the floor.

He saw a speck of dim light, closed his eyes and prepared for a rough landing.

A moment passed. Then another. Then two more.

No splat…? Stitch Head thought. He opened his eyes. He was swaying gently, suspended in the middle of the dungeon, one metre in the air. The rope had gone taut.

The Creature had caught him!

But had Arabella seen him?

"Double crossin', stink smellin', stitch-faced good-for-nothin'…"

Slowly, Stitch Head turned towards the dungeon door. Arabella was slumped against it, butting her head repeatedly on the wood.

"Kick him from here to Drubbers Dollop…" she said with a sniff. She no longer sounded angry, but sad. Stitch Head's guilt at having locked her up immediately redoubled. It was all he could do not to apologize there and then. But her fate … the fate of the orphans … the fate of the entire castle was at stake.

He tugged once on the rope.

It didn't move.

He tugged again, more sharply.

Still no slack.

What are they doing up there? Stitch Head thought. He checked Arabella hadn't moved, and then glanced over to the table. There were the potions. He stretched his arm until he thought his stitches might pop, but still his fingers barely brushed the edge of the table. The potions were out of reach.

Stitch Head shook his head – there was nothing else for it. He carefully began untying the rope around his waist. After some considerable fiddling, he released the knot and he dropped to the floor with a

THOD.

Stitch Head froze. After a moment he dared to look back at the door. Arabella was still, her head resting on her knees. He breathed a silent sigh of relief and crept over to the table. He reached under it and took out his potion bag. Then slowly, gingerly, placed a bottle inside. Then he took a second bottle, and placed it on top.

KLINK!

He looked around again. Arabella had not moved. He placed another bottle in the bag.

KLINK!

Again, he checked on Arabella. Then he took two more bottles and slid them carefully into the bag.

KLINK!

KLINK!

Almost there, he thought. He glanced up at the dungeon door.

Arabella was gone.

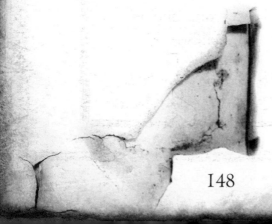

STITCH HEAD VS ARABELLA
(Breaking bottles)

MAD MUSING No. 690

"Friendships come and go;
madness lasts forever."

From *The Occasionally Scientific
Writings of Professor Erasmus Erasmus*

"AAAARGH!" Arabella roared, leaping out of the darkness and pouncing on Stitch Head. "Lock me up, would you! I'll kick your stinkin' stitches off!"

A panicking Stitch Head slipped out of her grasp and scuttled across the floor.

"I thought we was friends!" shouted Arabella, grabbing Stitch Head's potion bag. "But we ain't, 'cause friends don't lock each other in dungeons!"

Stitch Head darted behind the table. He saw the curtain cord, still dangling from the listening trumpet ... but Arabella blocked his route.

"You're just trying to get rid of me!" Arabella roared. "All you care about is them Little Terrors! You was just looking for a way to get rid of me, just like everyone does!"

"That's not true!" whimpered Stitch Head.

"I-I just want to help you!"

"I don't need no help!" Arabella cried. She shook for a moment, as if fighting back tears. "I thought you was different, Stitch Head. I thought you and me was friends."

"We are!" replied a desperate Stitch Head. "Th-that's why I want to cure you."

Arabella hardened before his eyes. She took a deep breath.

"You've got a cure for everything and every*one*, ain't you?" she hissed. "Well, I don't need curing! And I don't need your stinkin' potions!"

Arabella took a bottle out of the bag and threw it. Stitch Head ducked as it flew over his head and smashed against a wall in a spray of green liquid.

"Wait!" Stitch Head pleaded, but Arabella threw another bottle, and another, emptying the bag as she dashed the potions against the walls of the dungeon. Stitch Head huddled behind the table as she cried out in rage.

"I wish I'd never set foot in this stupid castle!" Arabella shouted, throwing the empty bag to the floor. Then she turned her attention to the table.

"Arabella... No!" Stitch Head cried, but it was too late. With a wild, swinging kick, Arabella upturned the table, sending the rest of the potions smashing to the floor with a

KRASSSH!

Stitch Head dived for cover as thick plumes of multi-coloured smoke filled the dungeon. He made a dash across the room, sliding under Arabella's legs and leaping for the cord.

"Creature! Ivo! Pull! Get me out of here!" he shrieked, wrapping the cord around his wrist. He tugged twice. "Pull! Pull now!"

When nothing happened, he turned back to see Arabella walking slowly towards him, a wild look in her eye.

"You all reckon I'm a beast..." she snarled. "Fine! I'll be a beast!"

Arabella leaped at Stitch Head, as the cord was suddenly yanked up, pulling Stitch Head into the air! He felt Arabella grab his leg and the pair of them were pulled inside the trumpet. Arabella barely fitted inside, but the cord was pulled with such force that they were dragged upwards at speed.

"Wait! She's got me, stop pulling!" cried Stitch Head, desperate not to unleash the Beast of Grubbers Nubbin on the world again. He tried to let go of the cord, but it was wrapped tightly around his wrist. Within moments, Stitch Head and Arabella popped out of the top of the trumpet and fell into a heap on the library floor.

"SORRY, Stitch Head!" cried the Creature, holding the cord in its claws. "Ivo HANDED me the END of the cord just in TIME … but then I COULDN'T remember if it was ONE tug or TWO…"

"Hello, Angry Girl!" said Ivo. "Did Stitch Head cure you of beastliness?"

Arabella stood up, walked slowly over to the Creature, and kicked it hard in the shin.

"Don't look like it, does it?" she said, as the Creature hopped around, holding its leg. "Reckon I know when I ain't wanted. You lot have yourself a nice almost-life, Little Terrors 'n' all. I'll take my chances in Grubbers Nubbin."

"But ... it's *nightfall*," said Stitch Head, glancing out of the window at the gloom. "You're going to change!"

Stitch Head flinched as Arabella reached out towards him. She thrust her hand inside his collar, grabbed his key and yanked it from around his neck.

"You know what?" snarled Arabella. "I reckon I could *do* with a change."

With that, she stormed out of the library.

"Arabella, wait!" cried Stitch Head, trying to untangle himself from the cord.

"Don't WORRY," said the Creature, resting a comforting claw on Stitch Head's shoulder. "I'm sure this will ALL have blown OVER by the MORNING."

"What? How is this going to— This is not going to blow over!" cried Stitch Head, throwing the cord to the floor. "Arabella's going to turn into the beast and attack Grubbers Nubbin! Again!"

"Hmm … you PROBABLY should have LEFT her in the DUNGEON," added the Creature.

"I didn't *mean* to— Never mind," Stitch Head sighed.

He left the Creature and Ivo in the library and raced through the castle. He finally caught up with Arabella as she stormed across the darkening courtyard towards the door.

"Arabella!" Stitch Head yelled. "Please don't open that—"

They both skidded to a halt.

The Great Door was already open.

Again!

THE NINETEENTH CHAPTER

THE OPEN DOOR

(More figures, more fog)

Grubbers Nubbin Notice Board

AFEARED OF THE BEAST?

Don't let frantic debility confine you to th' faintin' couch! Take a bottle of

DR STIFFNECK'S NERVE RIGHTIN' TONIC

And get back to your baking!

Available from Grubbers Nubbin Town Hall

"So tell me, Stitch Head," began Arabella, "how did I open the door if I didn't have no key and I was locked in the dungeon?"

"I-I don't know…" Stitch Head muttered.

"Well, why don't you stand there like a fish and *mullet* over," Arabella huffed. "I'm going to get to the bottom of this and clear my name!"

She threw Stitch Head's key to the ground and raced out of the open door.

"Wait!" Stitch Head cried. He picked up the key, locked the door behind him and sped after her.

Grey-black clouds moved quickly across the night sky, obscuring even the brightest star. A thick blanket of fog clung to the grass. Stitch Head followed Arabella down the hill as she ran towards Grubbers Nubbin, questions racing through his mind. If she didn't open the Great Door, who did? There were still so many unanswered questions ... could he risk trusting Arabella?

"Arabella! Please wait, I—" Stitch Head began, as he caught up with her.

"Don't even talk to me," Arabella snapped. "As soon as I find out who's really behind this mess, I'm leaving for— Wait! There!"

She pointed down the hill. Ten paces in front of them were two figures scurrying through the fog towards Grubbers Nubbin, one slightly ahead of the other.

Two human children.

Arabella redoubled her pace. Stitch Head tried to keep up, but it was no use. There was nothing he could do but watch as she pounced, colliding with the children and sending them skidding down the hill.

"I knew it! I knew it was you!" Arabella howled, grappling with the children. "Now stop squirming or I'll bash your teeth!"

Stitch Head squinted in the gloom, trying to make out who it was. Then a familiar voice rang out across the hill.

"Unhand me, you mad thing!"

"*Cuthbert?*" blurted Stitch Head. Arabella had the squirming Cuthbert helpless in a headlock. In the other arm, she held Cuthbert's feeble sidekick.

"L-l-let me go ... p-please!" Squit wheezed, trying in vain to escape her grasp.

"Shut your noise-holes!" Arabella growled. "See, Stitch Head? Didn't I say this was all Cuthbert's doing! He's a pilfering pork pie!"

"Pilfering? How dare you!" Cuthbert declared. "I'm innocent! I-N-O-S-E-N-T!"

"Liar! You pinched my key and stole that potion from the prof's lab!" shouted Arabella. "*And* I'll bet my boots you planted that bottle in my pocket! You're the beast! You're going down to Grubbers Nubbin to feed your fat face!"

Cuthbert! Could he be the beast? thought Stitch Head. He certainly looked well fed compared to the other orphans. But if Arabella was the beast, wouldn't she want to pin her crimes on someone else? Stitch Head pressed his fingers to his temples, his head bursting with questions.

"You mad thing! I am not a thief, and I am not a beast!" Cuthbert howled, helpless in Arabella's grip. "I'm only out here because I was *following him!*"

Cuthbert pointed a chubby finger at Squit.

"L-let me go!" Squit cried.

"I don't understand..." said Stitch Head.

"Yeah, don't pass the buck, y'louse-eared robber! He only does what you tell him!" snapped Arabella.

"So I thought!" cried Cuthbert. "But then I saw Squit sneaking out to the courtyard! He unlocked the Great Door! *He's* your key thief! I was pursuing him down the hill when you *assaulted* me..."

"Is … is that true?" asked Stitch Head. Squit stared at him for a moment, a look of desperation in his eyes. Then he reached into his pocket and took out a large iron key.

"You see?" sneered Cuthbert. "Squit purloined it from your pocket after you showed it off! Never show a key to a thief…"

"I'm sorry," Squit said meekly. "P-pickpocketing's what I d-d-do…"

"Squit, you half-pint bandit!" snarled Arabella, releasing Cuthbert and tightening her grip on Squit. "What's this all about? Tell me or I'll twist your head off!"

"There's no time — you have to l-l-let me go," begged Squit, becoming increasingly anxious.

"I got locked in a dungeon 'cause of you!" Arabella retorted. "You ain't goin' nowhere 'til you fess up! And don't leave nothing out!"

Squit struggled and squirmed but it was hopeless. He looked at Stitch Head with a desperate, pleading look.

"After I t-took the key, I followed you to the rafters," he began. "You were t-talking about stealing from the town. I was *s-s-so* h-hungry. I thought of going to Grubbers N-n-nubbin myself … but I was afraid of getting c-c-caught…"

"Wait, you were there with us in the rafters?" Stitch Head muttered. "Then you must have heard us talking about— Oh *no*."

"I thought it would m-make me strong and it tasted like chocolate," said Squit quietly.

"I d-didn't m-mean to t-take it … it just happened. N-now that … thing comes every night…"

"What thing? What you on about?" Arabella snapped.

"Arabella, let him go…" said Stitch Head. "Let him go now!"

"T-too late…" said Squit, looking Stitch Head straight in the eye. "It's t-t-too late… Now the B-BEAST is coming."

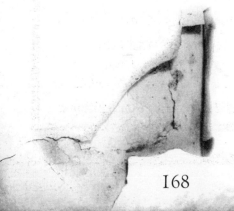

CHANGING TIME

(The beast is back)

MAD MUSING NO. 677

"Embrace change! Especially if
it involves claws and fangs."

From *The Occasionally Scientific
Writings of Professor Erasmus Erasmus*

"Wait, *you're* the beEAAAAH—" yelped Arabella as Squit threw her off like a dog shaking water from its coat. Cuthbert, too, ended up sprawled on the ground.

"I t-told you to let me go!" yelled Squit, rocking from side to side, his head in his hands. "Too late!"

The crunch-crack of shifting bones echoed through the night air as Squit began to change. His body stretched and contorted in every direction. His tiny hands grew into huge, sharp claws. His eyes burned white, and his teeth were replaced by large grey fangs. In moments he had grown to ten times his size and sprouted thick black fur all over his body. In a matter of seconds, the skeletal Squit was no more ... there was only the Beast.

RRRRR...

Stitch Head backed away as the beast fell on to all fours, growling loudly.

"Squit, are … are you in there?" he said quietly.

RRROOOOOOWWWRR!

The beast roared and flicked out a great claw, sending Stitch Head skidding along the ground. By the time he'd recovered his senses, the beast had turned towards Grubbers Nubbin and loped into the fog.

"Squit! Come back here and apologize for your wilful deception this instant!" cried Cuthbert, as the beast's growls echoed through the air.

"That sneak must've planted the potion bottle on me back at the castle, right when I was beating him up," added Arabella. "The nerve!"

"Arabella, I'm … I'm so sorry," said Stitch Head, rushing over to her and helping her to her feet.

"Why?" she grumbled sarcastically. "'Cause you didn't trust me or 'cause you locked me in a dungeon?"

"Both! All!" replied Stitch Head. "This is all my fault. I have no potions … I have no plan. I don't know what to do."

Arabella saw the desperation in Stitch Head's eyes. She sighed and scratched her head.

"I could try kicking it, I s'pose," she said.

"Ha! Why, the mad thing's a genius!" laughed Cuthbert sarcastically. "J-E-E-N-E-E-U-S!"

"I don't see you coming up with no smart ideas!" growled Arabella.

"Me? What am I supposed to do? I've just

found out my dearest sidekick is a monster!"
Cuthbert declared. "I don't mind telling you,
this whole experience has left a bad taste in
my mouth…"

"Bad … taste…? That's it!" cried Stitch
Head. "I have a plan! Well, sort of… Come
on! We have to get back to the castle!"

ATTACK OF THE BEAST

(Cakes vs pies)

Grubbers Nubbin
Notice Board

Join us for a fun day of barricade building!

Keep out the beast and make friends!

(Non-attendance frowned upon)

"It's the beast! The beast is back!"

The cry rang out across Grubbers Nubbin. Lookouts on rooftops spotted the beast emerge, snarling, from the fog. It was confronted by an impressive barricade constructed from bricks, wood, furniture and horse carts blocking its path into town.

The beast roared defiantly at the sight of the obstruction. It charged, throwing the full force of its monstrous weight against the barricade.

Again and again the beast attacked. For a while, it seemed as though the barricade would hold, but with each relentless assault it began to weaken. Long minutes passed, but the beast did not stop.

"Blimey! It's goin' to break through," cried one of the distraught townsfolk.

"Protect the pies!" howled another.

"Never mind the pies! Protect the cakes!"

"It ain't going to eat your cakes over my pies…"

"I'll 'ave you know the beast ate twelve of my cakes last night. I was bakin' all night to replace 'em."

"Is that so? Well it ate *thirteen* of my pies."

"Only 'cause your pies are so measly small. They wouldn't fill a baby's gut!"

"Would you two shut up? The beast is breakin' through!"

RRROOOOOOOWWWRR!

With an almighty howl, the beast crashed through the barricade, sending rubble flying. It bounded through the town, following its nose down the main street to the town hall, its eyes burning in the night, its hunger consuming it.

It was met by an army of townsfolk, blocking its path to the hall. They brandished pitchforks, torches and a host of makeshift weaponry.

"You ain't getting our feast, beast!" cried one of the burlier townsfolk, brandishing a plank of wood.

"Not even the tiny pies!"

"You shut up about my pies!"

"Jab it!"

"Stab it!"

"Kill it!"

The beast reared up on its hind legs, howling defiantly. It swung its claws, swatting two of the townsfolk through the air. Others flung burning torches, striking the beast's hide. It roared again, shrugging off the flames, before charging into the crowd and knocking the townsfolk about like skittles. The beast hammered against the door of the town hall, desperate to break through. In moments, the door began to splinter…

"Oi, beast!" came a sudden cry. "Don't fill up yet! We've got your feast right here!"

The beast turned. The townsfolk turned.

Twenty paces down the street stood an odd ensemble of humans and monsters. At the forefront, the familiar, wild-haired Arabella cracked her knuckles. Next to her stood Cuthbert, straightening his tie. The Creature loomed over them, cradling the cooking pot of Stuff in its two biggest arms. Upon the Creature's shoulder sat the tiny, one-armed form of Ivo. And behind them, barely noticeable in the grey-black gloom, was Stitch Head.

"Are you SURE about THIS?" asked the Creature, placing the pot of foul, bubbling Stuff on the ground, as Stitch Head tied the long curtain cord around his waist.

"Not in the least, but unless anyone has a better idea…" muttered Stitch Head. The group gave a collective shrug. Stitch Head sighed and pulled the cord tightly. "Arabella, Cuthbert … are you ready?"

"Can't blinkin' wait," snarled Arabella.

"This is positively the worst idea ever," declared Cuthbert.

"Whatever it takes," whispered Stitch Head. He took a deep breath, and held it. Then the Creature picked him up, and dropped him into the Stuff.

PLORP!

TO DEFEAT THE BEAST

(Roar emotion)

MAD MUSING NO. 50

"Keep calm and make monsters."

From *The Occasionally Scientific Writings of Professor Erasmus Erasmus*

Stitch Head felt himself sucked helplessly into the Stuff. The Creature held tightly to the end of the curtain cord as it was pulled in with him.

The beast let out an angry BLEH! as the foul smell reached it. The townsfolk, too, began to wretch at the unbearable odour.

"Oi, beast, you hungry? 'Cause I've got a pair of kicking boots that I'm going to feed you!" roared Arabella.

"You are nothing but a boy in beast's clothing!" added Cuthbert. "A coward hiding behind flashy fangs and bad breath!"

RRRRR...

"I could kick the beast out of you in my sleep! You ain't even worth waking up for!" Arabella continued.

"You misleading miscreant!" shouted

Cuthbert. "You would rather others suffer than take responsibility for your own failings!"

RRRRRR...

"Snot-neck!"

"Weakling!"

"Stink-burp!"

"Deceiver!"

The beast reared up once more, consumed with rage, and let out an almighty

RROOOAA~!

"Now!" shouted Arabella. With an almighty wrench, the Creature yanked the curtain cord, dragging Stitch Head out of the burping ooze with a

FLOOOOORP!

Stitch Head emerged, caked in a thick grey layer of Stuff. The Creature immediately swung him over its head – once, twice, three times around – then flung Stitch Head towards the beast as it roared! The beast's angry howl still filled the air as Stitch Head flew through the sky, straight towards its open mouth.

ROOAA-ULP!

The beast clamped its jaws shut, its eyes burning with confusion.

It had swallowed Stitch Head whole.

IN WITH THE GOOD, OUT WITH THE BEAST

(That's the Stuff)

DON'T BE BEATEN BY THE BEAST

Chug a bottle of

MRS PIMPLECHIN'S SWIGGIN' SAUCE

Fortifies the body and strengthens muscles.
One chug and you'll be
stronger than a monster!
Guaranteed results every time!

(Results not guaranteed)

Arabella, Cuthbert, the Creature and the gathered townsfolk watched in silent disbelief as the beast cocked its head, unsure as to what had just happened. The curtain cord hung loosely from its mouth. A long moment passed.

RRR...?

"Uh, NOW what?" said the Creature.

"Stitch Head did not explain next part of the terrible plan," said Ivo nervously.

"I *said* it was the worst idea ever," sighed Cuthbert.

"Come on, Stitch Head, where are you?" whispered Arabella.

Suddenly, the beast's stomach let out a loud, wet grumble. Then another ... and another ... and then, finally:

RRRR!

A torrent of grey-green vomit spewed forth from the beast's mouth! It flew through the night air, showering the townsfolk with foulness, but their fearful cries were drowned out by the sound of the beast's grim expulsions. It dug its claws into the ground, its head flinging helplessly from side to side as vomit arced through the air.

RUUUUURRRGH!

"Eat *that*, beast!" yelled Arabella. As the townsfolk retreated, the beast stumbled forwards, slipping and sliding on slime escaping from its mouth. Then, as it flailed upon the ground, it began to change. Its thick black hair fell from its body ... claws retreated into hands ... fangs became teeth ... the transformation was over in a matter of moments. Where once stood a hulking monster, now lay a slender human child, shivering and cold.

The Beast of Grubbers Nubbin was no more.

"We DID it!" cried the Creature. "IS THAT what we were TRYING to DO?"

Arabella raced over to the pool of still-bubbling vomit and dragged out a whimpering Squit.

"Not … h-h-hungry … any more…" he moaned, holding his stomach.

"Take him!" Arabella cried. She helped Squit to his feet, then handed him to Ivo and Cuthbert as they waded into the slime. "Now where is he…?"

Arabella lifted the curtain cord out of the slime. She followed it into the foulness, sliding her hands through the cord until…

"Got him!" Arabella pulled Stitch Head out of the spew and cradled him in her arms. "You all right, Stitch Head? Wake up!"

Stitch Head lay still, his head lolling limply to one side.

"Wake up, I said!" Arabella growled, shaking him. "Ain't you never been swallowed by a monster before?"

"Arabella?" said the Creature, looming over them. "IS he—?"

"He's fine!" she snapped, shaking Stitch Head again. "You're *fine*, Stitch Head ... now wake up!"

Sttich Head remained still. Arabella gently wiped the ooze from his face.

"Don't you dare do this," she said quietly.

A long moment passed. Arabella pulled Stitch Head closer.

"I mean it," she sniffed, squeezing him tightly. "I ain't had chance to forgive you yet. And if you don't wake up, I ain't never forgivin' you ... *ever*. So don't you—"

"Guuuh!"

Stitch Head sat up with a start, his eyes wide with horror.

"Stitch Head!" cried Arabella.

"You're ALIVE!" shrieked the Creature happily. "ALMOST."

Stitch Head wiped the slime from his eyes and saw Cuthbert tending to a dazed and queasy Squit.

"Did … did it work…?" he uttered.

"Yeah," said Arabella, wiping a tear from her eye. "Your terrible plan worked ... and you stink worse than ever."

"That was GREAT!" declared the Creature, scooping Stitch Head up in one arm and the pot of Stuff in the other. "Let's do it AGAIN!"

FOULNESS AND FORGIVENESS

(No place for humans)

Grubbers Nubbin
Notice Board

No notices until
further notice.

S titch Head and company beat a hasty
retreat from Grubbers Nubbin. Confused,
suspicious murmurs echoed through the air
as they hurried back up the hill. A few of
the townsfolk even questioned why there were
children accompanying the monsters, but
in the end everyone was so covered in beast
vomit that no one was sure who was human
and what was monster.

No one looked back as they made their way up the hill to Castle Grotteskew. Even Cuthbert, painfully aware that he was within reach of a building full of food, could not muster an appetite. Instead, they listened to a rueful Squit tell his terrible tale of transformation.

"I'm sorry I p-planted the p-p-potion bottle on you," he said to Arabella, as they finally reached the castle. "I thought if anyone f-found out I was the b-b-beast, I'd be l-locked up forever."

"Lock you up for being a beast?" Arabella replied, shooting Stitch Head a look. "Now who'd do a nasty thing like that?"

"Arabella..." muttered Stitch Head, but in truth, he didn't have the energy for much more.

"Everyone make a mistake," said Ivo, from the Creature's shoulder.

"And at LEAST there was no HARM done," added the Creature, tying not to spill the Stuff as it sloshed about in the pot.

"No harm done? Squit turned into a rampaging monster! And nearly destroyed that town!" shrieked Cuthbert. "And he didn't even save any food for me!"

Stitch Head, Arabella, the Creature, Ivo, Cuthbert and Squit spent the remainder of the night scrubbing themselves clean. By the time they reunited in the castle's dining hall, the sun had risen over the horizon, banishing darkness and fog.

"S-so you're sure I won't ch-change again?" Squit asked Stitch Head.

"Do not worry – if you do, we will launch Stitch Head into your mouth again! No problems!" said Ivo.

Stitch Head and Squit both shivered at once.

"I just can't BELIEVE the Stuff SAVED the DAY!" declared the Creature, replacing the pot of Stuff in the corner of the room. "I make better POTIONS than Stitch Head!

ACTUALLY, I think I was MADE to be a MONSTER MEDICINE MAKERER. I've finally found my CALLING…"

"*I* can't believe I'm ever going to get this otherworldly whiff off me," tutted Cuthbert, sniffing his arm in disgust. "The foulness!"

"Arabella," began Stitch Head quietly. "I really am sorry. I don't know if you can ever forgive me for … well, everything."

"Yeah, well, I reckon Squit played us both for mugs," she replied. She ruffled her hair, which looked decidedly odd for having had a good wash. "Not that I'm saying that's any sort of excuse for you not believing me, mind."

"It isn't! It isn't, you're right," Stitch Head began. "I should have trusted you. I'm sorry."

"Good," said Arabella. "'Cause it turns out I already forgave you last night. On account of you not dying 'n' all."

"You … you do?" blurted Stitch Head. "I mean, you did?"

"Yeah, well, maybe I ain't been my usual, reasonable self neither," Arabella said. "All the attention you was giving the Little Terrors … maybe I felt like I wasn't worth bothering with."

"Of course you are!" cried Stitch Head. "Arabella, you're … you're my *best* friend."

"Oi," said Arabella, giving Stitch Head a friendly punch on the arm. "Don't get all soppy on me."

Stitch Head immediately felt as if a weight had been lifted from his shoulders.

"As much as I hate to break up this festival of fawning and flattery," began Cuthbert, "there is still the *tiniest* problem of a hundred hungry orphans, due to wake up any minute now with groaning stomachs."

"Do you *always* have to point out the obvious?" grumbled Arabella. She turned to Stitch Head. "We managed to cure Squit of being a full-blown beast. I reckon we'll find a way to take care of the Little Terrors."

"What are you saying?" asked Stitch Head.

"I'm saying that if you want the orphans to live here, that's all right with me," Arabella replied. "Even Cuthbert."

Stitch Head smiled as wide a smile as he could muster. But it didn't last long.

"No, you were right, Arabella," he said, gravely. "Potions and monsters and madness ... Castle Grotteskew is no place for humans."

"So what are *you* saying?" asked Arabella.

"I so wanted to keep my promise – to keep the orphans safe, to give them a home here in the castle – that I put everyone in danger," Stitch Head said. "And as bad as it got, it could have been a lot worse, for the orphans and for the castle. I can't risk it happening again."

He walked over to the wall, took the dinner bell off its hook, and rang it with all his might.

CLANG-A-LANG-A-LANG-A-LANG-A-LANG-A-LANG!

GUZZLIN' DAY

(Belonging)

MAD MUSING No. 995

"Humanity is an experiment
upon which I must improve."

From *The Occasionally Scientific
Writings of Professor Erasmus Erasmus*

So it was that this year's Guzzlin' Day was a little different. The townsfolk of Grubbers Nubbin would remember three things above all:

One, that they had, the previous night, repelled a monstrous beast and saved the feast.

Two, that the Guzzlin' Day sun shone particularly brightly.

And three, that they were joined by one hundred hungry orphans, who appeared out of nowhere, with nowhere else to go.

―――――――――――――

"What's happening, Arabella?" whispered Stitch Head. He, Arabella, Ivo and the Creature (cloaked in a pair of dining-hall curtains) were hiding behind an upturned horse cart, part of the wreckage of the blockade on the outskirts of town.

Only minutes ago, they had led the orphans out of the castle and down the hill. Then they had left them to continue into Grubbers Nubbin on their own.

"Arabella? Can you see? Is it working?" asked Stitch Head. "Are the townsfolk taking them in?"

"Looks like it, more fool them. Cuthbert's laying it on pretty thick," she huffed, peering out from behind the cart.

Stitch Head dared to sneak a peek and saw the people of the town gathering round the horde of children. He was sure he saw Cuthbert look back at him and wink.

"Help us, do! We poor orphans have been wandering for days!" Cuthbert cried, already holding court. "Oh, who deliver us from adversity? Who will save us from starvation?"

It wasn't long before the townsfolk's bafflement turned to compassion, which then became the warmest of welcomes.

"Oh, you poor, lost babies!"

"Come an' warm yourself by the fire!"

"Have some pie!"

"But leave room for cake!"

Stitch Head, Arabella and the Creature looked on as the townsfolk took the orphans under their collective wing, treating them as if they were honoured guests. Soon, the children were enjoying an open-air feast as fine and filling as they could ever have imagined. They ate until they could eat no more – and still found room for cake.

"You know what? I reckon the Little Terrors will be just fine," said Arabella.

"Yep! I PROMISED them a FEAST and they GOT one, JUST like I had absolutely

NO idea might actually HAPPEN," added the Creature. "GOODBYE, awfuls, DON'T think because we KICKED you out of the CASTLE that we don't think you're GREAT."

Stitch Head just sighed.

After a while, Stitch Head and his friends snuck back to the castle. Arabella unlocked the door and pushed it open. She stopped for a moment in the castle entrance.

"Them pies did smell good," she said. "And the cakes, for that matter."

"Now I am really wishing I had a nose," sighed Ivo.

"I'm sure they'd have you back, Arabella … if you wanted," said Stitch Head. "I mean, you are *from* Grubbers Nubbin."

"I s'pose…" Arabella said. "Though I'd

probably have to stop kicking so many folk and watch my blinkin'—"

"SWaaaRTiKi!"

Arabella glanced up to see her monkey-bat, Pox, finally dare to swoop down from on high and land on her shoulder. It gleefully started to chew her hair.

"You know what? If it means I can hang around with monsters, I reckon I'd rather eat beetles," she said. "Anyway, I ain't never belonged in Grubbers Nubbin."

"You don't have to," said Stitch Head. "You already belong in the castle, with us."

"Yeah," she said, ruffling her hair. "I reckon I do."

A KNOCK AT THE DOOR

(More where that came from)

Little Terrors,
Little Terrors
We miss you now you've left
But by golly it is quiet
So we don't feel too bereft

Signed,
The Creations of Grotteskew

By the time darkness had descended upon Castle Grotteskew, almost-life was back to almost-normal. The creations had, for the most part, come out of hiding into the moderately less dark shadows.

But no one particularly seemed to miss the wild, human clamour.

No one, strangely, except Stitch Head. For him, the orphans had meant the chance for things to be different ... the chance for him to feel more than almost-alive. But in the end, what else could he have done?

Castle Grotteskew ain't no place for humans...

Stitch Head looked over to Arabella. She sat in the corner of the dining hall, lazily tickling Pox's belly, as her own stomach rumbled loudly.

"We have to do something," he whispered to the Creature. "Arabella can't live like this, on ... on beetles."

"AND the occasional dead CROW," insisted the Creature, stirring his pot of hateful Stuff.

"*Exactly,*" said Stitch Head. "If we don't find—"

KLUNG!

KLUNG!

It was a knock at the Great Door. Stitch Head froze. The creations froze. In fact, only Arabella didn't freeze.

"I'll go then, shall I?" she groaned, hopping to her feet. "I swear, if it's an angry mob I'm going to kick every last one of 'em in the nose, stupid blinkin' humans..."

"Wait!" said Stitch Head, as Arabella paced huffily out of the dining hall. He raced after her, reaching the Great Door as she unlocked it. "Arabella, Stop! Don't—!"

But Arabella was already pulling the door open.

They peered out. The bright moon illuminated the night sky, and fog rolled slowly down the hill. And far off, in the gloom, Stitch Head could have sworn he saw two figures scurrying down the hill.

"Is that…?" he began, as Arabella looked down. By her feet was a small basket, wrapped in a tea towel. A folded piece of paper sat atop the basket, upon which was written ARABELLUR.

She picked up the note and unfolded it.

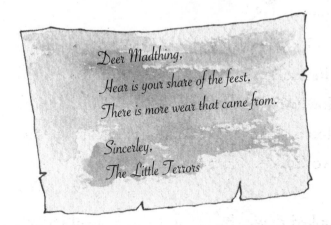

Deer Madthing,
Hear is your share of the feest.
There is more wear that came from.

Sincerley,
The Little Terrors

"That Cuthbert can't spell for a bag of toffee," she tutted. Then she unwrapped the tea towel and looked inside.

It was a pie. A warm, freshly baked pie.

"Well, ain't that something," she said with a sniff. She lifted the pie from the basket and took a slow, deliberate bite into its golden crust. She could not stop the smile that spread across her face. In that moment, Arabella was as happy as Stitch Head had ever seen her.

He dared to reach out a tiny hand and placed it upon hers.

"See?" he said. "Maybe humans aren't so bad after all."

Have you read...

In CASTLE GROTTESKEW

something BIG
is about to happen...

...to someone SMALL.

Join a mad professor's forgotten
creation as he steps out of the
shadows into the adventure
of an almost-lifetime...

Guy Bass

STITCH HEAD

The Pirate's Eye

Someone SMALL
is about to set sail
on a **BIG** adventure.

Join a mad professor's forgotten
creation as he prepares for an
almost-life on the high seas...

Guy Bass

STITCH HEAD

The Ghost of Grotteskew

Someone SMALL
is about to discover a
BIG secret.

Join a mad professor's
forgotten creation as he fights
for his heart and soul...

Guy Bass

Stitch Head

The Spider's Lair

Someone **SMALL**
is about to get
into **BIG** trouble.

Join a mad professor's forgotten
creation as he gets caught up in a
web of mystery…

VISIT THE AUTHOR'S WEBSITE AT:

www.guybass.com

STRIPES PUBLISHING
An imprint of Little Tiger Press
1 The Coda Centre, 189 Munster Road,
London SW6 6AW

A paperback original
First published in Great Britain in 2015

ISBN: 978-1-84715-609-9

Printed and bound in the UK.

2 4 6 8 10 9 7 5 3 1